STARS
IN MY
CROWN

STARS IN MY CROWN

BY JOE DAVID BROWN

DECORATIONS BY GOULD K. HULSE JR.

WILLIAM MORROW & COMPANY, NEW YORK, 1947

NOTE: the characters of this book are completely fictional and any resemblance they may bear to actual persons is coincidental. The same is true of the events described. Parts of this book have appeared as stories in *The Saturday Evening Post*.

To

FRANCES

With Whom I'm Living Happily Ever After

I

WOMEN were still weeping over the graves at Gettysburg when my grandpa came to Walesburg. Nobody knew where he came from or why he came. He just showed up one night in a store-bought blue-serge suit and eased his way into Jere Higham's place.

Grandpa walked quietly to the end of the bar and put down his Bible. He didn't have to call for silence because it followed him through the long smoky room like a hound dog. Grandpa cleared his throat and began to speak. "Boys," he said, "I'm your new preacher and I aim to give my first sermon right here."

A couple of General Lee's men, still in uniform, began to laugh. Grandpa didn't even glance that way. He just reached under his long coat and pulled up two long-barreled cavalry pistols and slapped them on the bar.

"Either I speak," he said, "or these do!"

Nobody crossed my grandpa after that. They stood quiet and listened. Even Old Jere Higham stood quiet and still while Grandpa interrupted his business. And when it came time to pray, he took off his flour-sack apron and bowed his head with the rest. That was the gift my grandpa had. When he preached you couldn't help but listen. It was his voice mostly. It wasn't how he used it, but what he had behind it. My grandpa had conviction. Sometimes when he preached it seemed like thunder and lightning were blazing around the room. Other times he spoke so softly and simply that everybody wept.

But always Grandpa preached about one thing. It was the Golden Rule. No matter how he changed it around, Grandpa always told people to do unto others as they would have others do unto them. That was his belief. That was his creed. That was his weapon against evil.

Not many folks knew it, but the sermon Grandpa gave in Jere Higham's that night was the first one he had ever preached. It rang true because his faith had been forged in the heat of a score of skirmishes and battles. Grandpa knew a lot about wars, and about people who fought them. He had been one of Quantrill's Guerillas, and most of the men he had fought with were as unchristian as they were bold. After a while people said harsh things about Quantrill—Southerners as well as Yankees. Grandpa wouldn't take sides one way or the other.

Grandpa almost never talked about the war and he had grown mellow and soft-spoken by the time I got

8

big enough to run by his side more than thirty years later. He always wore black, my grandpa did; and he stood tall and erect. He had white hair and it curled down around his collar. He wore black string ties and big broad-brimmed hats. His eyes were as blue as a quarry pond on a clear day, except when he was angry. Then they seemed to freeze into two chunks of blue ice.

As far as I know, Grandpa never raised his voice when he was angry. He would just draw himself up to his full height, and his voice was clipped and his lips almost disappeared. I remember the first time I ever saw him that way. A salesman was beating a livery-stable horse down by the covered bridge one day. When Grandpa saw him, his face flushed and his jaw muscles stood out like knobs. He reached up and took the whip from the fat little drummer's hand.

"Stranger," he said, "that's a good hoss. He don't balk without reason. You better go in that bridge and find out what's wrong."

The drummer started to say something, but Grandpa looked at him with those hard blue eyes of his, and he thought better of it.

He eased out of the buggy and waddled into the covered bridge. A few seconds later we heard his frightened yelp. His face was purple when he came out panting.

"Rattler," he gasped, "bigger'n my leg!"

My grandpa swished the whip and looked at him coldly. "Stranger, I could drive you back in there."

The sweating man looked startled, then frightened. "No! No!" he said.

Grandpa looked at him for a full minute. Then he walked into the bridge and with one slash of the whip cut off the rattler's head. He came back and handed the drummer seven rattles and a button.

"Stranger, keep these in your pocket, and whenever you hear them rattle, remember—do unto others as you would have them do unto you."

He walked away a few steps, with me churning my little fat legs to keep up and almost splitting with adoration. Then he turned for a parting shot at the uneasy little salesman.

"And that means hosses and dogs—and all God's creatures."

Things like that made me awfully proud of Grandpa, but then, almost everybody in Walesburg felt the same way. It was a little town but it had a big way of doing things. Grandpa's church was an example. The people gave it to him after he had been in Walesburg for three years, preaching around in saloons and houses, and, on occasions, even barns. The church sat on a little rise over by Brown's Springs. The people loved it because it was part of them—part of their lives and built with their sweat.

If ever a church was put together with loving hands, that one was. Times were hard then. Nails cost a dollar apiece and the only dollars around Walesburg were signed by President Jeff Davis. All of them together wouldn't have bought a single nail. Labor wasn't cheap either. It couldn't be bought at any price. But it was the most plentiful commodity around Walesburg.

The church was Old Gene Caldwell's idea. He

brought it up one Sunday night while Grandpa was holding services in Clem McCullough's parlor. Old Gene had lost an arm at Bull Run, and after benediction he got up fidgety and nervous in the lamp light.

"Hol' on," he said, "hol' on, Ah got a matter to bring up." Folks stopped sort of surprised. Old Gene choked a bit, but he was bound and determined to go on. "Ah bin checkin' around," he said, "and Ah find we got three saloons in this town and nary a church. Somehow it jest don't seem right. How come the drinking folks has got a place to drink in whilst we don't have a place to pray in?"

Grandpa knew right away what Old Gene was thinking, and his heart leaped. But he didn't let on. He had never mentioned a church because Grandpa always felt that you could force a man to do almost anything except support God. That had to be a freewill offering.

Grandpa looked at Old Gene's red face. "Churches cost money, Brother Caldwell."

Gene shook his head. "Money ain't nuthin', Parson. It don't take money." He held up his one good arm in that quiet parlor. "Ah gave one arm to the Confederacy. Ah guess it won't hurt me none to dedicate the other one to the Lawd."

Clem McCullough spoke up then. "Ah got a shed full of split pine shingles and myself and three sons to help put them on."

Henry Abernathy was next. "Ah got some well-seasoned ridge poles and Ah got six sons and four daughters who ain't afeered to work for the Lawd."

That was the way it was. Every man there searched

his mind and his soul and he found he had something to offer toward a church. Soon the little congregation was bright-eyed and bubbling over with things to offer. Then Granny Gailbraith spoke up. She was old and wrinkled and she remembered seeing Andy Jackson when she was a girl. She spoke low in a cracked voice. "I can't offer anything for a church, Parson, except my prayers. I aim to do that right here. I want to pray that I'll live to see a church in Walesburg."

Everyone got quiet and still, then they went to their knees and offered up a prayer for the church. That was the firm foundation for Grandpa's church. Sweat and callouses were the dollars and cents that paid for it.

Nearly everybody in Walesburg took a hand. The men cut down the straight young pines in the bottom lands for flooring. They sent up into the hills for the biggest oaks for the joists and beams. And the nails— that was the difficult part. The women and children made them, shaping them lovingly out of the pieces of hard oak and ash.

Right behind the church site Gene Caldwell started building a windmill. Work went sort of slow on account of Old Gene's one arm, but he wouldn't allow anyone else to help. When the windmill was finished it stood as a mighty fine monument to Gene's faith. It stood as high as any in the whole valley, and it would catch a breeze that was too slight to even start a ripple on Edward's Lake.

Even Granny Gailbraith had her split-cane-bottomed chair moved down amid the hammering and sawing. Her gnarled hands whittled out the last wooden

1 2

nail. It was carried up to Grandpa and he drove it into the block supporting the cross on the steeple.

Then the folks moved into the church. It still smelled of pine and oak and cedar. They prayed and Grandpa preached. I asked him once what he said.

"I can't rightly remember," he said, "but it had to do with usin' God's property. I told them that we had taken a part of God's land and the things which grew on that land to build a monument to Him." He mused a moment. "Just an ordinary sort of sermon, I guess. Just a plain 'Thank you, God.' There wasn't any use goin' into a long-winded talk on *why* we were thankful. God could look at our sweaty clothes and blistered hands and know that."

Other churches were built in Walesburg after that. They built them out of stone and bricks. They brought in polished pews from Louisville, and the Baptist church had a big stained-glass window which came all the way from St. Louis. Somehow, though, they never rivaled Grandpa's church for beauty.

City folks used to call it "quaint," and once a circuit-rider preacher who had gone to Harvard College came by and wrote it up in the *Southern Methodist Magazine*. Grandpa carried the clipping in his big black wallet and finally wore it out showing it to people. But that was before the Miracle of the Grindstone. After that, I guess nobody could keep count of all the stories. Even Gussie Lou Liles down at the library gave up after filling two composition books. But that all came later.

II

GOD must have intended my grandpa and grandma for each other. If He didn't, He must have been mighty pleased when He looked down and saw them together. Grandma had a gentle touch, and while Grandpa liked to move fast and get things done, she could come along quietly and smooth down the rough edges.

My grandpa was always gentle with people, but especially so with Grandma. It was easy to see why. Grandma was made for gentleness. She had white hair, and she was frail, but not a bit brittle looking. I always thought she was sort of like a fluff of dandelion down, just sort of precious looking. Even when she scolded me, it always sort of seemed that she was smiling inside.

I never knew my mother. She died the same week

I was born, and my father, a proud, jealous man, went away to New York. He came back only once, and I don't remember that very well. I was about three and I was sleeping soundly when he and Grandma came into my room. I was cross and fretful when they woke me up. About all I remember is that Grandma was holding a lamp, and she smiled gently when my father picked me up and held me close. He smelled of tobacco and leather and shaving soap. He snuggled me close for only a minute and by the time he put me back in bed I must have been asleep again. Before the year was out he had died in a Florida training camp. All the memories I have of him are the way he held me that night, and a picture he sent me, looking proud and tall in his Spanish-American War uniform.

It used to give me a guilty feeling that I wasn't sorry my father went away. Somehow, though, it just wouldn't have seemed right if anyone had taken care of me except Grandma and Grandpa.

I told Grandma about this one time. It was a long, hot afternoon and we were sitting on the veranda. Grandma was tatting and I was stretched out on the floor, wiggling my toes. Suddenly, it just came to me how happy and peaceful I was. I thought about it for a while, and before I realized it, I guess I sort of blurted it out:

"Grandma, I'm glad you and Grandpa are my real folks . . . I mean . . . I mean . . . I'm glad I live with you 'stead of a mama and poppa, like other boys."

Grandma stopped tatting as quickly as if I had

snatched the shuttle from her hands. She sat looking at me a whole minute, and I felt so ashamed for saying such a thing that I got red in the face.

Tears filled my grandma's eyes. Then she got up and leaned over and kissed me real quick and went into the house. It made me feel bad at the time. It was a long time afterward before I learned that women also cry when they are happy.

My grandma had been married for forty-odd years but I never heard her call my grandpa by his first name. When she was speaking of him to other folks she usually called him "Parson Gray." To Grandpa's face, she called him "Mister Gray." This seems odd now, but it didn't when Grandma said it. Somehow it just seemed natural. Maybe it was because she didn't like Grandpa's full name. It was sort of formal at that. The sign on the church said: "Josiah Doziah Gray, Pastor," but most of the time Grandpa just signed his initials. Everybody called him Parson.

Grandpa used to grin when Grandma told me stories of the days when they were courting. He wasn't afraid to walk into General Grant's guns, or to jump astride a horse when it was at full trot, but he admitted he always got tongue-tied when Grandma was around.

Besides that, Grandpa was just a poor preacher, struggling along with a new church, and my grandma's family owned the biggest plantation in Jones Valley. My grandma had everything she wanted when she was a girl and plenty of rich young men always came calling.

Then, too, my grandma was a heroine of the war, even though she was just a little girl. It went back to the time Yankee soldiers came through the valley, shooting livestock and burning houses and barns. My grandma's father, Old Colonel John Scott, was off fighting with General Lee, and most of the slaves had run off before the Yankees got as far as Taylor's Ford.

One day when the bluecoats were so close that the people in Walesburg could hear the sound of their muskets, my grandma's mother sent her three oldest daughters off to the hills. She kept my grandma, who was twelve, with her. The two of them were frightened and white-faced but they worked as fast as they could, dragging china and furniture and food into the kitchen.

The Yankees were so close that the hooves of their horses could be heard when Grandma's mother remembered a barrel of sugar in the smokehouse. "Quick, Harriet," she said, "we must get that sugar."

They ran out to the smokehouse, with their hearts thumping with fright, and looking over their shoulders, expecting to see the Yankees at any moment. They wheeled that big barrel of sugar into the kitchen. Then Grandma's mother climbed up on the barrel, and sat there scared but determined. My grandma held close to her skirts.

First they heard the sound of saddles creaking and the rough voices of soldiers. Then there was the sound of firing as the bluecoats shot the few remaining pigs and an old blind mule. The woman and the little girl huddled closer when they heard a man's footsteps on the back veranda.

It was a big, bearded Yankee sergeant who came into the kitchen. He barely glanced at Grandma and her mother. He went back to the door and bawled: "Aw right, men, in here! Clean it out!"

Then he walked over to the pair huddling on that sugar barrel. "Les' see wha'cha got there," he said.

My grandma and her mother didn't say a word, just huddled closer. "Aw right," said the sergeant, "git off! Move off there." My grandma and her mother didn't budge. The sergeant gave the woman a little push. She sat stiff and defiant.

Then the sergeant got mad. Without another word he slapped my grandma's mother right across the face. He wasn't a bit prepared for what happened.

My grandma was on him like a hawk. She scratched and kicked with every bit of strength in her slight body. The sergeant was so surprised he stood there with his mouth open. Then he gave way. He had been in the saddle for days, and his clothes were thick with dust. Every time my grandma hit him, heavy, yellow dust rost up in clouds. It almost blinded him.

He started for the door. When he did, my grandma grabbed up a saucepan and started pounding him with it. About that time, the sergeant, almost blinded with dust, and having swallowed his chew of tobacco in the first fury of Grandma's attack, started bellowing and coughing as though he were fighting a whole platoon of Confederates.

The Yankees outside heard the noise and came running. Before they could reach the door, it fell open. Out tumbled the sergeant, with my grandma whacking him where it did the most good. The other Yankees couldn't make out what it was all about at first on account of the dust. Finally they saw it was a twelve-year-old girl with long curls pounding the sergeant. Some of them fell on the ground they laughed so hard.

The young lieutenant in charge came up about that time. My grandma said he didn't laugh, except in his eyes. He reached down and took the saucepan from my grandma's hand. She gave it up easily, because she was exhausted anyhow.

The lieutenant looked down at the sergeant, still lying choked and surprised on the ground. "Sergeant, how do you expect to get back to Illinois, if you can't protect yourself from a rear attack?"

Then the lieutenant turned to my grandma and made a grave, little bow. "Miss Rebel," he said, "if you learn to cook in that pot as well as you dust off sergeants —you'll make some man an admirable wife."

Then the lieutenant turned to the laughing soldiers. "Mount up!" he said. Some of them looked surprised but they grinned and went to their horses. My grandma watched them drive down the road, and when they got to the bend, the lieutenant turned and waved.

My grandma used to smile slyly and cut her eyes at Grandpa when she got to that part of the story. He would always do the same thing, clear his throat with a sort of snorting "Hurrmmph!"

Grandma was seventeen and had a lot of beaus when she met Grandpa and he came to her house to dinner. After that night she said she never had any doubt about how it was going to work out.

"How—how did you know, Grandma?" I asked one night while we were sitting on the veranda.

"Because I loved him," she said.

I sat still there in the night and turned that over in my young mind. Finally I asked, "How can you tell when you're in love, Grandma?"

Grandma sat rocking quietly and she sort of smiled. She cocked her head and listened to Grandpa walking the floor in his study and mumbling over next Sunday's sermon.

She leaned over and patted me on the head. "John," she said softly, "nobody can tell you about love. But I promise you—when it comes, there'll be no mistakin' it."

III

AUNT PIM was my grandma's sister, and she was the only one who still lived at the Scott home on the edge of town. Aunt Pim was an old maid but she knew more about love than lots of folks who married and had big families. By way of speaking, my Aunt Pim's whole life was dedicated to love. Almost nobody in Jones Valley could understand that because Aunt Pim's love wasn't dedicated to a man at all. She was in love with a memory—and a tree.

It wasn't an ordinary sort of tree. It was an oak, a towering, big oak. Even people who laughed at Aunt Pim admitted that as long as she had to pick a tree, she certainly couldn't have done better. It grew at the south end of the veranda at Aunt Pim's sprawling house, and even folks who never noticed trees particularly used to stare at it. On Sunday afternoons nearly everybody who had a buggy used to drive out Westfield Road, past Aunt Pim's house. No matter how fast they came wheeling up the road, they would always rein up their horses when they came abreast of Aunt Pim's. They'd pass by very slowly, gawking at the tree.

Sometimes some of the young folks would laugh, but nobody minded because young folks will laugh at anything when they are out riding on Sunday. Even Aunt Pim used to smile sort of gentle-like when she heard them cutting up as they passed by.

Aunt Pim always sat on the veranda on Sunday afternoons. Almost every Sunday after I got big enough to walk out to her house, I used to sit with her. I loved Aunt Pim, but the main reason I started going, I guess, is that she would let me take off my church shoes.

Shoes cramped my feet something terrible. Sometimes it seemed like they would burn my feet off before Sunday School and morning services were over. My grandma wouldn't let me take my shoes off on Sunday, but Aunt Pim didn't mind. I'd sit on the veranda with her, pressing my feet against the cool floor, while she hand embroidered handkerchiefs. Every time we heard a buggy coming up the road, Aunt Pim would hold her needle still, and I'd stop shuffling my feet until it passed by. Sometimes they would stop. We'd enjoy that most of all, especially if it was a family.

Usually it would be the mother who explained. "Look, children, look up there near the first branch. See it? See that sword? No, no, Jere, down lower—down just below the first branch. See? That's a sword blade,

That's a cavalry sword blade—the kind your grandpa carried when he fought the Yankees."

And then we would hear a child's treble: "How did the sword get there, Mama?"

Women's voices always sounded just a little bit breathless when they started telling the story of the sword in Aunt Pim's tree. "Well, children, once upon a time—a long time ago, a young cavalry officer was in love with Miss Pim. When he got his orders . . ." Then, Aunt Pim and I would hear the man cluck to his horse and the story was lost in the sound of the buggy wheels.

That was the way it was, and I didn't mind. Nobody could tell the story of the sword as well as Aunt Pim. She told it like it was supposed to be told.

Aunt Pim was just seventeen when the first cannonball landed on Fort Sumter, and the oak was just a slender sapling, scarcely bigger than a man's wrist. It wasn't even as big as Ahman Hall's wrist because he was the strongest man in the valley. He was strong and he was handsome. He had curly auburn hair and flashing teeth. He was fiery like all planter's sons, but my Aunt Pim knew how to handle him.

It was easy to see why. My Aunt Pim was older than Grandma, but somehow all men remembered their manners when she was around. Even cranky Old Bob Ware who ran the hardware store was gallant when she came in. He used to run to open the door for her, and bowed and scraped so much that other customers used to stand around open-mouthed.

Maybe it was because the way Aunt Pim looked— all neat and trim. Maybe it was the way she carried her slim shoulders or the tilt to her gray head. Whatever it was, it wasn't at all hard to imagine how she had looked when she was a young girl.

It wasn't hard to imagine how much she loved Ahman Hall either. She could tell it so well. "When I used to see Cap'n Hall ridin' up the path to my house, I would stand on the veranda with my heart beatin' faster and faster. I do declare when he came up the steps I used to hol' my throat because I was afraid my heart would leap right out and fall at his feet."

Aunt Pim had been in love all right. She and Ahman Hall went everywhere together. And people who used to see them out riding or dancing a reel said that it was wonderful that two people could find so much to laugh about when they were together.

They would have been together always, I guess, if the war hadn't started. But it did start, and my Aunt Pim wasn't the only woman who wept in her pillow because her man was going away. Captain Hall looked awfully handsome the day he came to say good bye. My Aunt Pim was in the rose garden when she saw him coming up the road on his prancing big bay.

Aunt Pim used to smile when she recalled that day. "I ran into the house like the wind," she said. "I looked worn out because I had been cryin' so hard, but I pinched my cheeks till they were bright as haw berries. Then I ran out to meet him."

Captain Hall came up the steps slowly, and he didn't take his eyes off my Aunt Pim's face. He went directly to her and took her in his arms, right out where everybody could see.

2 4

"Cap'n Hall kissed me then," Aunt Pim said, and even after more than fifty years the recollection brought a flush to her cheeks. "He kissed me . . . and I . . . I kissed him back."

Aunt Pim said she cried a little, too, and when Captain Hall saw her tears he grinned and asked: "What can I fetch you from Washington—when I come back next month?"

"I tol' him right out what I wanted," Aunt Pim said. "I tol' him, 'I want you to come back jes' like you are—I want you back . . .' "

They walked in the garden after that. What they said was Aunt Pim's secret. She always paused and smiled off into the distance when she got to that part of the story. Maybe they didn't say anything. Maybe Aunt Pim was just treasuring the touch of a hand . . . the sharing of a mood. Whatever it was, it made Aunt Pim dreamy-eyed fifty years later.

The lightning bugs had started blinking and the katydids had started singing when Captain Hall said he must leave. He and Aunt Pim walked slowly to the little oak where his horse was tethered. It was always easy for me to picture them there in that beautiful night. He was tall and handsome in his gray uniform and shiny cavalry boots, and she scarcely came to his shoulder. He untied his horse and then he kissed Aunt Pim again. It was a long kiss because it had to last a long time.

Then Captain Hall did one of those things that made him the kind of a man who won my Aunt Pim. He drew his sharp cavalry sword, and with one powerful, deliberate stroke thrust it through the little oak.

25

"There wasn't another man in the county who was strong enough to have done it," Aunt Pim said proudly.

Ahman Hall turned to my Aunt Pim in the twilight. He took her slender shoulders in his two powerful hands. His voice was low and intense as his young face.

"This sword was my father's and his father's, Pim—but now it belongs to both of us. It's going to be out here always . . . guarding our love. Watch it carefully, and keep it shiny. Leave it here until I get back."

Then Captain Hall sprang into the saddle and wheeled his horse into the night. My Aunt Pim stood silently by the tree. Her hand was on the hilt of that sword and big tears were rolling down her cheeks. She stood there until the sound of the horse's hooves were lost in the night. After that, she wiped her eyes, stuck out her bottom lip, and marched into the house—to wait.

I V

THAT summer wasn't quite the same. My Aunt Pim went to quilting bees and she rolled hundreds of bandages, each one with a prayer that it wouldn't be used. But that little oak tree was her life. She planted a rose bush by its base and it grew as steadily as her love. It was tended as well. Twice a day she went to the tree. It was always the same. She would water the rose bush, and then she would take a soft cloth and polish that sword. It fairly shone. Sometimes the sun would hit it full force and slaves working in the fields could see its brilliance a full half-mile away.

"Lawd, lookit that ole sword shine! Looks lak hits on fire. Looks lak hit belongs to the Angel hisself, guardin' the Garden o' Eden. Man! Oh, man!"

Then came Bull Run, and Aunt Pim shed a tear for every man who dropped there on Henry Plateau, or who was left cold and stark in the thickets. She waited days before a letter came, all fancy with flourishes and curley-cues. She ran out to the tree and she read that letter with her shoulder pressed against the hilt of the sword.

"What did the letter say—what did Cap'n Hall write?" I asked Aunt Pim once.

Aunt Pim looked sort of puzzled. "You know," she said, wrinkling her forehead, "I don't rightly remember. Cap'n Hall wrote that he loved me, and he wrote that he missed me, but I remember that day mostly because of another thing.

"I looked at that sword, and lo' and behold—I saw that tree was actually growing around that blade." She sort of smiled. "Guess it had been that way for a long time, but I just hadn't noticed. Anyway I was sur-prised. Always before, that tree and that sword had been two different things. Now they were one."

The Battle of Fort Donelson was next. Captain Hall's horse was shot from under him, but he managed to get through. When Aunt Pim got the news she went into the night and stood by the sword a long time. "No-body could understand that," she said. "But somehow I always felt that Cap'n Hall was awfully close when I

2 7

stood there. I reckon he was," she said a little shyly. "Leastways, I talked to him a mite."

Up until the Tennessee campaign started, most folks hadn't realized what it meant to be in a war. Then gradually, their way of life began to change. Old Ernest Mackay couldn't get any paper because of the times and he started printing the *Messenger* on old handbills and rolls of wall paper. Pretty soon he wasn't printing any news at all. That is regular news, like social doings and speeches made at the county seat. It took all of his paper and all of his time to turn out reports of skirmishes—and casualties.

People would gather outside the *Messenger* office every day. They would stand quietly and whispering like at a funeral until Old Man Mackay came limping to the door with his papers.

He would hand them out solemnly to a hundred eager hands. Sometimes there was a lot of smiling and cheering as the papers went from hand to hand. Sometimes grief hung over the dusty street like a black shadow. People would run their eyes down casualty lists with a dull dread. Aunt Pim knew all about it.

"I would get a paper and my heart wouldn't seem to beat until I had looked it up and down," she said. "I would look once—quickly; then I would feel my hands getting warm again, and I would look once more. This time I would go carefully. When I couldn't find his name I would feel sort of tired and worn out. I was happy—but not the kind of happy that makes you grin. It was the sort of happy that makes you want to pray."

As time went on, the sound of crying was heard

more often in that crowd outside the *Messenger*. Sometimes a woman would scream. More often one fainted. Or maybe an old man would stand shock-still, clutching a piece of flimsy paper in his rough hands, with big tears rolling down his cheeks.

Grief was an old story by the time another spring came to the valley. It was quiet, though, and the war seemed far away that April day Aunt Pim went to the tree. It was early and the sunshine was flooding down the side of Red Mountain in the distance. Aunt Pim carried a watering can, and she went directly to the rose bush and tended it carefully. Then, she turned to polish the sword. Her heart almost skipped a beat.

The sword was shiny, but the shininess seemed like a transparent film. Underneath there was a dark shadow. Aunt Pim's hands were cold and trembling when she started to polish the blade. She went carefully at first, polishing with long even strokes. When the shadow remained, she began to cry. She rubbed harder. Then panic seized her and she rubbed so hard that her young arms began to ache with the effort. She was sobbing now—sobbing and praying. But the shadow was deep—beneath the surface.

Finally, in her panic, she called out in a voice choked with sobs, and Big Tom heard her. Big Tom was the houseboy and he was around at the woodpile, chopping wood for the kitchen. He came running with worry written all over his handsome black face.

"Whass the mattah with yo', chile? Lawd, whass the mattah with yo'?"

"I just couldn't talk to him," Aunt Pim said. "I was

just cryin' and takin' on so. Finally he took the cloth from my hand and made me tell him what was wrong."

Big Tom couldn't see the shadow at first, but finally he did, and then he grinned. "Ain't nuthin' wrong with dat sword, honey. Ain't nuthin' wrong a-tall. Yo' jest been polishin' hit too much. Yo' can't polish hit so much. Yo' jest about to wear dat ole sword out with yo' polishin'."

Aunt Pim believed Big Tom. I guess she believed him because she wanted it to be true. Anyway, she quit crying. But the shadow on that sword was on her heart. That night she learned that the drums were beating a tattoo at Shiloh.

The sword seemed darker the next morning, but Aunt Pim couldn't be sure. She was standing in that breach of anxiety which always came when she knew Captain Hall was in battle. The news trickled back ever so slowly, and every day there were bigger crowds outside the *Messenger* office. People knew it was a big battle when the news came that General Johnston had been killed. But nobody was prepared for such big casualty lists.

The first lists came in the morning and my Aunt Pim pressed through the solemn crowd right up to the front door of the *Messenger* office. She could hear the clank of the old hand presses, and no matter how hard she tried, she couldn't be calm. The presses went clank . . . clank . . . clank. But to Aunt Pim, they went over and over again . . . Captain . . . Ahman . . . Hall . . . Captain . . . Ahman . . . Hall. . . .

It seemed hours before the presses stopped, and Old

Man Mackay limped to the door with his papers. They were printed on wall paper this time. It was yellow wall paper with pink cherries growing in clusters. Aunt Pim managed to get one of the first papers. She didn't look long. There were a hundred names. Aunt Pim saw one. She saw one, and she saw a tall, proud man in the twilight . . . and she saw the way his hair grew on his neck . . . and she heard his voice.

My Aunt Pim stood there alone in the midst of all those people. She didn't cry. The tears burned her eyelids but they wouldn't come. She stood there staring into the years. She stood still and numb, clutching that foolish little piece of gay paper to her breast. My Aunt Pim didn't have much left.

That was the way Aunt Pim's story always ended. After she told it I would sit still for a long time. I never thought to ask what happened after that. Maybe I knew. Aunt Pim just lived. She went on from year to year. She grew middle-aged, and then, she grew old. It was as simple at that.

It was sort of like the tree. It grew bigger every year, just like Aunt Pim's love. It was all she had and it stood like a sentinel outside her window. After a few years, the tree almost covered the sword. Forty years after the guns sounded at Shiloh there were only two feet of blade sticking out from the massive trunk.

Sometimes in the evening when I walked home from Aunt Pim's house, I used to try to imagine what it would be like when she met Captain Hall again. It would be wonderful, I knew . . . but already I was nine years old and I began to doubt if any man was worth it.

31

V

EXCEPT for my grandma and grandpa, nobody took care of me as well as Uncle Famous Prill. He wasn't my real uncle at all, because Uncle Famous was black and he had been born a slave. Sometimes I thought his mind never shook off the fetters. We were still-fishing for cats in Village Creek one day when I asked him if he was happy when Abe Lincoln set him free. He shook his handsome white head sadly.

"Lawd, chile, jest sayin' a good thing don't make hit true."

It was the first time I realized Lon Hamilton was causing Uncle Famous so much unhappiness, and it made me downright sad. I jiggled my line in the water a minute and looked at his grave black face and his heavy shoulders which sagged ever so slightly. He saw my concern and chuckled.

"Don't yo' go wastin' no sorrer on ole Uncle Famous. Watch dat line. Ah seed a big ole cat come a-sneakin' disaway jes' den. He seen me, too, and Ah know what he's a-thinkin'. He's a-thinkin', 'Dat ole man's too smart for me—but dat lil' boy . . . why, Ah'll jest grab his doughball and scat away.' "

Sure enough, I felt a tug at my line and as I jerked it hastily and fairly trembling with excitement, a lazy old yellow catfish went sailing over my head. I was on it like a hound on a possum while Uncle Famous shouted instructions.

"Cotch hit's head, chile, and watch out for hit's fins. Dat's a yallar cat, and eff'n hit fins yo', hit'll pizen yo'. Cotch hit's mouf, chile. Cotch hit's mouf!"

That was just like Uncle Famous. He had his sorrow, but he hoarded it deep within him. The feel of a fish wiggling at the end of a line, the sound of a pack of cold-blooded hounds on the trail of a fox, the sight of a coon snarling and snapping at the top of a hickory tree brought him happiness. He didn't bother anybody in Walesburg, and nobody bothered him, except Lon Hamilton.

At first, most folks didn't think that was any discredit to Uncle Famous because Lon was always fighting somebody. Nearly everybody in Walesburg was poor and they didn't seem to mind it. Lon was rich and his money weighed on him like a heavy saddle on a galled mare. I guess most folks wouldn't even have known they

33

were poor if Lon hadn't come along. But he did, and he started things humming. He bought a sawmill out on the edge of town and it was always screaming and groaning away, making him money.

Grandpa said that sawmill was the only thing in Walesburg busier and louder than Lon Hamilton. Grandpa used to chuckle a lot at Lon but he couldn't do it in front of people because of him being a preacher and preachers have to be dignified. But Grandpa never held back about letting people know which side he was on in the fight between Lon and Uncle Famous.

Lon started it all when he bought sixty acres of land out near Brown Springs and started digging for mica. He found it, too, and he made lots of money until the vein ran smackdab into Uncle Famous' rocky twenty acres. Lon rode over to see Uncle Famous one day and offered to buy his property, but Uncle Famous wouldn't sell. Lon went back again and again, and every time he raised his price. Uncle Famous wasn't interested.

Lon was fit to be tied. He went around making threats and frothing at the mouth. But there was nothing he could do. The property belonged to Uncle Famous outright and legal. He just didn't want to give it up.

Most folks couldn't understand that because Lon's offer finally got to be right handsome. If Uncle Famous had accepted it, he would have been the richest darky in the county.

One day while I sat watching Uncle Famous split shingles for his smokehouse, I asked him why he didn't take the offer.

34

"You could have lots of money, Uncle Famous," I said. "You could buy one of those store-bought rods and reels, and a new shotgun—and . . . and jest lots of things."

Uncle Famous stood still a moment with his axe poised over the wedge. He fingered the strap of his faded, clean overalls.

"Chile, how many suits of overhalls kin Ah wear at one time?"

"One," I answered, and he smiled.

"How many beds kin Ah sleep in at one time?"

"One."

"How many houses kin Ah live in?"

"One," I answered again.

"How many times a day Ah needs vittles?"

"One, er, ah . . . three!"

Uncle Famous swung back the axe and hit the wedge—wham! Then he straightened up and smiled at me.

"Ah got a suit of overhalls. Ah got a house. Ah got a bed. Ah gets mah vittles three times ever' Gawd's day. What for Ah needs that money, chile?"

I couldn't answer that. I guess nobody else could have, if it hadn't been for Lon. He had the answer to everything, and when he talked lots of folks listened. Even some of the good folks favored him, but mostly it was the riff-raff down at Jere Higham's place. At times he sounded downright convincing.

"That black coon is holdin' up the progress of this heah community," he'd shout and his face would get all red and flushed. "Ah offered him mor'n a fair price for that broken-down lan'. Ah ain't one to take advantage of a houn' dawg. Ah pay fair and Ah talk fair. The black coon is jest gettin' too uppity."

Lon would stand in the center of the floor, waving his fat little arms and pretty soon more and more people were nodding in agreement whilst he jawed away.

"Ah see it thisaway," he'd say. "You men kin use some part-time work to tide you over 'til plantin' time, and Ah kin use you. There's lots of work to be done on that vein—a heap of work, an' Ah pay fair wages. You gonna deny your chil'lun and women folks on 'count of a black nigger?"

Lots of folks who never even thought of working for Lon Hamilton would nod when he said that.

I told Grandpa about Lon's gabbing while we were sitting on the veranda one night. Grandpa said Lon put him in mind of an old fox hound he once had named Big Black. Grandpa said Big Black was one of the best dogs in the county, but he was conceited. He just couldn't stand to have another dog get ahead of him. When Big Black was turned loose in a pack, he'd start baying the minute he picked up any kind of scent.

"That houn' had a mighty persuasive voice," Grandpa said. "He'd yowl and beller so convincin' that first thing you know, all the young dawgs would chime in for fear they couldn't trust their own noses. After the pups got to screechin', the old dawgs would join in, too—slowly at first, then louder and louder. Guess they were gettin' old and didn't want to admit it.

"Big Black had an advantage too, 'cause houn's jest

naturally like to bay." Grandpa settled back with a sigh. "Folks are the same way, I guess."

"What ever happened to Big Black?" I asked.

Grandpa chuckled. "Carried a whole pack of houn's right smack into a brood of polecats one night. Wasn't a dawg in the county that could breathe halfway decent for a week. Big Black was the hardest hit. His eyes were swollen shut and you could smell him comin' a half mile away. None of the other dawgs ever trusted him after that. Barkin' up the wrong tree once was enough for them."

Grandpa sat quietly for a minute. Then he spoke sort of low, like he was thinking out loud. "Guess Lon Hamilton will have to stir up an awfully big stink 'fore he's satisfied."

It didn't take long. The new corn was about as high as a ground squirrel when the big trouble started. It had been raining all morning and I was sitting on the back veranda when I saw Uncle Famous unlatch the back gate. I knew something was wrong. He walked with a stoop and he looked sort of sad.

"Uncle Famous!" I shouted and went flying to meet him. He smiled a little bit but not in his eyes.

"Mawnin', chile. Is yo're Grandpa to home?"

Grandpa had heard me shout and he called from the door for Uncle Famous to come in. It was plain the old man was carrying a passel of trouble by the time we settled in Grandpa's study. He didn't say much but fumbled in the pocket of his faded overalls and handed Grandpa a piece of paper.

I peeked over Grandpa's shoulder as he read it. Somebody had printed in big block letters:

"Get off this land, Nigger. This is your last chance! Get off this land or get a rope around the neck. If you can read this run. If you can't read run anyhow." Down at the bottom somebody had drawn a big cross, and it was signed "The Night Riders."

Grandpa studied the note a long time. The longer he looked the tighter his jaw got. Finally he handed the note back to Uncle Famous.

"Where did you get this?" he asked.

"Hit war stuck to mah door dis mawnin'," Uncle Famous said. "Didn' hear nobody come up in the night. Warn't no soun' a-tall. What hit mean, Pawson? Why those folks wanna bother a ole man lak me? Ah bin livin' on dat farm nigh on forty yars. Hain't give nobody no trouble. Don' aim to give no trouble now. Why they bother me, Pawson?"

Grandpa sat still for a long time, and I could tell by the far away look in his eyes that he was thinking hard. Finally he turned to Uncle Famous.

"You afraid of these people, Famous?"

For the first time Uncle Famous grinned. "Lawd, no, Pawson, Ah ain't a-scared. Thar ain't a full-grown man in Walesburg Ah ain't knowed since he was as little as this heah chile." He turned and put a gnarled hand on my shoulder.

Grandpa stood up. "Then you go home, Famous, and forget this foolishness. But you come back to see me Saturday morning. Don't you worry. You've got nothin' to worry about."

Grandpa was wrong about that. About midnight on Friday forty or fifty men showed up out at Uncle Famous' place. They wore white sheets and they had masks made from flour sacks. They sneaked up through the woods and banged on the door to Uncle Famous' cabin. When he came out, two of them grabbed him and held him tight. The others came up dragging a big cross made of split pine and wrapped in croaker sacks soaked in coal oil.

They didn't say a word. They just held Uncle Famous tight while this cross was set afire. When it burned down, one of the Night Riders came up to Uncle Famous and pinned a note to the front of his overalls. Then they left just as quickly and as quietly as they came. There wasn't a word spoken.

Uncle Famous wasn't hurt none, but he was plenty shaken when he showed up to see Grandpa the next morning. His face was drawn, and he shook his old head slowly.

"They means hit. Ah jest cain't unnerstan' hit, Pawson. Ah jest cain't unnerstan' hit!"

He handed Grandpa the note the Night Riders had left. It was grim. "This is your last chance. You have one week to get off this land. Make tracks, Nigger! Get off or get off feet first at the end of a rope! We mean business!!!" There was the same crude cross at the bottom and it was signed: "The Night Riders."

Grandpa read the note and stood there and folded it neatly before handing it back to Uncle Famous. Then he reached for his old broad brimmed hat. "Make yourself at home, Famous, and wait heah until I get back."

I didn't even ask Grandpa if I could go along. I doubt if he knew I was churning along by his side. He didn't look right nor left, but headed straight for Lon Hamilton's office above Beggs Hall. Once he reached there, he went up the stairs without breaking his gait. I brought up the rear, all panting and breathless.

Lon was sitting with his feet on the top of his old rolltop desk when Grandpa came busting into his office. He swung his feet to the floor and looked kind of surprised when he saw us. But just for a second. Then his fat face lit up in a smile, showing all his gold teeth. "Howdy, Parson, draw up a chai . . ."

Something about Grandpa's face made him stop. Grandpa looked tall and stern and his blue eyes never left Lon's flushed face.

"Mr. Hamilton," Grandpa said, "the decent people in this community won't stand for the connivin', contemptible, bullyin' schemes your men are up to."

Lon looked flustered. "Now wait a minnit, Parson," he said. "Ah won't pretend Ah don't know wha'ya talkin' about. That nigger's jest bin actin' pigheaded, an' Ah reckon self-respectin' folks ain't gonna stan' for that. He's a-beatin' them outta money, that nigger is; an' Ah reckon some of the boys is pretty riled up about it." Lon finished a little lamely because Grandpa had nailed him with his eyes, and when Grandpa's eyes looked like that, it sort of made shivers run up and down your back.

He didn't appear to have heard what Lon said. He just started speaking very calm, but there was ice on every word. "Mr. Hamilton, I'm a servant of the Lord.

40

It's my business to save souls, but I'm also goin' to save people when they are worthy. I'm givin' you fair warnin'. Call your men off that old man. You're not goin' to misuse him. You have my word for that, suh, and if I wasn't a servant of the Lord I'd take a buggy whip to you."

Then Grandpa turned and walked out while Lon stood there open-mouthed. He followed us to the top of the stairs calling out: "Now lookit, Parson . . . Now, hol' on a minnit . . ." but Grandpa didn't look back.

We went straight to the house, with Grandpa not slackening his stride a bit. Uncle Famous was waiting for us in the study and Grandpa turned to him with a smile.

"Are you scared now, Famous?"

Uncle Famous stood a minute, turning his battered old hat in his hands, but he looked Grandpa straight in the eyes. "Ah ain't a-scared, Pawson."

"Do you want to sell?" Grandpa asked.

Uncle Famous shook his head slowly. "Nawsuh, eff'n Ah dies, Ah wants to do hit on my properitty."

Grandpa stuck out his hand. "All right, Famous, we'll see this thing through. Go home and wait for me."

V I

ABOUT sundown on Tuesday, Grandpa and I got ready to walk out to Uncle Famous' place. Grandma had a worried look in her eyes when she walked with us to the front gate, but all she said was, "Take care."

Grandpa and I walked slowly up the dusty road and darkness overtook us before we had gone halfway. It wasn't real darkness, though, because the moon was shining so bright it threw our shadows on the road. Uncle Famous had a hot meal waiting and, after we had eaten, we sat on the front steps. He and Grandpa did all the talking, and there wasn't a mention of the trouble. I guess I was the only nervous one. I sat and looked at the shadows in the woods and around a clump of haw trees in front of the house until it seemed the Night Riders were all about us.

When it came time for bed Uncle Famous insisted that we take his big four-poster, but Grandpa would have none of it.

"I slept on the groun' for four years when I fought for Gen'rl Lee," he said, "and I guess I can stan' one night on a pallet."

So Grandpa and I curled up on a tick feather bed on the floor and I guess he slept real well. I didn't. Every little sound made my heart go pitty-pat, and my palms got sweaty every time a board squeaked or a varmint made a noise in the woods.

We were up with the sun, but Uncle Famous didn't go to the fields. He didn't do any work that day, except cook and slop the pigs and feed the chickens. He and Grandpa sat on the front stoop most of the day and talked about old times in Walesburg and about different people they both knew.

The moon came up so bright that night that we could see it even before the sun went down. It was almost as bright as day, and as Uncle Famous' noisy old clock chimed off the quarter hours, he and Grandpa talked lower and lower. Finally they stopped talking altogether, and everything seemed sort of heavy . . . and waiting . . . and still.

Finally, Grandpa spoke: "Famous, will you go put on your Sunday clothes?"

Uncle Famous got up without a word and went into the cabin. It took only a few minutes, and then he came back, wearing his shiny, black suit. He had on a white shirt and a black string tie, and when I saw him with the moon shining on his white head, I knew what

Grandpa meant when he said Uncle Famous should have been a king. He joined us on the stoop and we sat still and silent while the katydids and the tree frogs chirped and that beautiful night grew older.

Suddenly I felt Grandpa tense, and looking off across the fields, I saw them! It was a frightening sight. My throat went dry. I wanted to run and hide. There were so many, just walking straight and determined and not making a sound. The moon shone on their white sheets. They didn't seem to have heads—just two black holes for their eyes. They seemed to be from another world. I was scared—so scared that my hands were cold. I could feel my heart beating in my throat.

When they were about twenty yards from the cabin, they stopped. The four white figures in front lighted pine torches. Then, without a word, they moved forward again.

Grandpa sat still until they were almost to the front stoop. Then he stood to his full height.

"Evenin'," he said.

You could almost see the surprise ripple through that crowd. It halted it dead for a moment. But just a moment. A voice in the rear hollered out: "Yo're a-wastin' yo're time, Parson. Stan' aside!"

Grandpa just sort of shrugged his shoulders and stepped to one side. I guess I gasped. I know I was so ashamed that the blood came rushing to my face. Two of the Night Riders grabbed Uncle Famous and another one put a rope around his neck. The rope had been ready all the time. It was big and thick and had a long ugly knot in it.

44

They started to hustle Uncle Famous off the porch when Grandpa spoke. He talked low because there was no need to talk out loud and he sounded sort of confused.

"Before you men go," Grandpa said, "I'd like to make my position clear in this matter. I didn't come out heah to try to talk you out of this thing. I want you all to know that. I'm a servant of the Lord and forty years of preachin' have taught me that you can't buck a group of determined men. I don't take part in politics, and I don't take part in arguments. That isn't my business."

That sort of halted things and you could almost feel the relief in that crowd. Tears were in my eyes and I wanted to cry. I was that ashamed.

Grandpa made a gesture, like he was asking for understanding. "I came out heah tonight because Uncle Famous Prill heah asked me to come. He knows he's got to die, and like everybody else he wanted to get things straight with God before he goes."

Somebody in the crowd shouted out: "Yo' kin say that again, Parson!" and a little wave of laughter swept the crowd, but it was nervous and forced.

Grandpa sort of smiled apologetically. "Be that as it may, I was asked by Uncle Famous to help set everything right. We've prayed together and we've talked together. Uncle Famous has even made a will and I have it heah." Grandpa reached into his big side pocket and pulled out a sheaf of papers. He slapped the papers against his other hand. "Heah's the will, and it's all legal and witnessed!"

You could see that set that crowd up right smart

There was just one thing on everybody's mind. Just who was going to get that farm and its mica vein? They all knew Uncle Famous didn't have much else.

Grandpa cleared his throat sort of legal-like. "Now, men, jest so there can't be any arguments about this, I'd like to read this will right heah in front of Uncle Famous so you can see it's legal. After you all hear it, and know that it's really his, you can go about your work."

Half a dozen voices spoke out consent to this.

Grandpa nodded a little thank-you, cleared his throat and stepped back into the circle of light from the cabin door. As an afterthought, he stopped. "I took this will down in Uncle Famous' own words. It isn't in lawyer form, but jest as he spoke it. I hope you understan' that." Then, he began:

"I ain't been able to lay much by in my life, but the things I have, I want to go to my friends. I got forty dollars in the Farmer's and Merchant's Bank and I want to leave it to Mistah Ernest Caldwell. The day he was bawn, his daddy took me in to see him, all wrinkled and red. I wanted to give him something then, but I didn't have nuthin'. I hopes he takes the forty dollars, even eff'n it is thirty years late. My fishin' poles I leave to Mistah Clem Shelton. I teached him to cotch sun perch when he was a lil' boy. He never had much luck. Ah tole him it was because Ah had a magic pole. His eyes usta shine at that. Maybe now he can cotch some fish.

"Mah rusty ole steel traps Ah leaves to Mistah Rufus Belsher. They ain't much good, but when Mistah Belsher was about eight he usta say he was goin' to the Naw'th Woods and be a trapper. Maybe now he can learn his littlest boy to cotch muskrats. Ah sure wants Mistah Perry Lokey to have my watermelon patch. He was a full-grown man 'fore he quit snitchin' mah melons and he knowed Ah seen him, too.

"That double-barrel'd ole shotgun o' mine, Ah leaves to Mistah Lem Parsons. When he was a lil' boy he shot hit off at a cottontail, and hit knocked him plumb over a rail fence. He's big enough and man enough to handle hit now."

There wasn't a sound in that crowd as Grandpa read. It was just still and quiet, and then I noticed a strange thing. Grandpa was reading, but nobody was looking at him. Every eye was on Uncle Famous. And it was Uncle Famous' voice they heard, just the way he talked, although his lips weren't moving. He just stood there, looking into the night with that big rope making his shoulders sag ever so much more. He was just looking into the night.

His will rolled on: "My hawgs Ah leaves to Mistah Thad Hankins. How that boy did love barbecue! Weren't hardly possible to cook hit without him comin' aroun'. Ah hopes he has a big barbecue and invites all our fren's. Mah tools Ah leaves to Mistah John Gailbraith. He allus liked to help me sharpen mah axe, an' Ah reckon now he's the best sawmill boss in the world."

Uncle Famous' will went on and on, and, then, a strange thing began to happen. Men in that crowd began to nudge one another. They didn't take their eyes off Uncle Famous, and it sounded like his voice instead of Grandpa's.

Uncle Famous didn't forget many people in that

47

will of his, and as he parceled out his few possessions, he had a little story to tell about every man. Bill Hicks got his razor. Taylor Mackay got his trotlines. Justin Beggs got his chickens, and there were just lots more.

Finally Grandpa came to the last page. He read very slow now, and his voice was heavy and melodious. "Ah wants all the isin' glass on mah proper'ity to go to Mistah Lon Hamilton. Mistah Hamilton wants that isin' glass pow'ful bad, and now he kin have hit. Ah leaves him all he kin find on mah farm. Ah allus foun' hit a bother mahself. Thar is something else Ah wants to leave Mistah Hamilton. Ah wants him to have mah Bible. Hit ain't fancy Ah guess. Hit's almost wore out, but Ah wants Mistah Hamilton to have hit. Ah hopes he reads hit."

That was all. That was the will of Famous Prill. Grandpa stopped reading and just stood there.

Nobody made a sound. Nobody moved. Grandpa spoke real low: "You can have him now, men." Somehow it sounded like a benediction. The pine torches had flickered out, and all the noises of the night closed about us. Then one man moved. He stepped up to Uncle Famous and took the rope from his neck. He threw it down like it was dirty and then turned and headed straight back through that crowd. It made way for him, and then, gradually, it began to dissolve. There wasn't a word spoken. The men just went away slowly and quietly.

Big tears were running down Uncle Famous' old face. He turned and shook Grandpa's hand. "Thank yo', Pawson." Then he laid a hand on my head and

48

went into his cabin. Grandpa reached for his handkerchief, and when he did Uncle Famous' will fell to the floor. I reached to pick it up. As my hand touched the white pages, I gasped. The pages were blank. Just four pieces of white, unmarked paper.

"Grandpa," I began, "this isn't a wi . . . !"

Grandpa looked down quickly. He took the papers and stuffed them into his big pocket. Then he smiled sort of calm-like.

"Yes it is, son. It's the will of God." Then he took my little paw in his big hand and we walked into the night while the katydids sang about us.

VII

CRAZY Ella really wasn't crazy at all. Grandpa always said that she just had a burden too heavy for her to carry. I guess Grandpa was right. Leastways, I was always glad I wasn't one of the kids who used to hoot and holler at Ella when she came pushing her baby buggy up Main Street.

Not that I think it would have made any difference to Ella. She never even looked around when the kids would chant: "Crazy Ella, Crazy Ella's got an empty bug—gy! Crazy Ella, Crazy Ella's got an empty bug—gy!" Maybe Ella didn't know the buggy was empty, or maybe it was like Grandpa said; she did know and just didn't want to admit it to herself. Whatever the case, the whole town helped Ella play her sad little joke.

It wasn't hard for the grown-ups to do, and sometimes I thought that the kids didn't jeer at Ella as much in mischief as they did from habit. Ella was a small plump woman and her face was as open as the little angel's on the cover of the hymn books in Grandpa's church. She was as neat as a milk pail and she kept her little house on the edge of Walesburg the same way. When I first remembered seeing her she had been pushing her buggy for fifteen years and it was the only thing that caused strangers to stare at Ella.

She was neat; her house was clean and well kept, and she went about her business like anybody else. But that buggy was as disordered as her mind. It was made of wicker and once it had been white but the years had cracked and peeled the paint. The wheels were rickety and when they turned it sounded like a nest of mice. Ella never went anywhere without the buggy.

Grandpa and I used to meet her often when we were out walking. Grandpa would take off his broad-brimmed hat and he and Ella would talk a while. The conversation was never any different from the ones Grandpa had with other members of his church until we got ready to leave. Then Grandpa would ask: "And how is the baby, Miz Wiley?"

At that, Ella's eyes would light up and she'd tell Grandpa about the baby. Sometimes it had the croup, sometimes it was teething and had been a little fretful, but always Ella would bend over that weather-beaten buggy and cluck and coo to her baby. That always made me feel bad because Ella didn't have a baby. That buggy was as empty as her hopes.

It always had been, even when it was new and

shiny and had come straight from St. Louis. But it was different in those days, because then Jim Wiley was alive and he and Ella expected to have a baby to put in it before long. They were especially happy because they had been married for ten years and it was to be their first child. The whole town was as happy as Jim and Ella, and the buggy was a present from the men down at the peanut-oil mill where Jim was foreman.

When time drew near for Ella to have her baby, people began to realize that she was going to have to pay a pretty heavy price for motherhood. Her health wasn't good at all, and old Doc Harris started calling more and more often. Jim took a lot of time off from the mill to stay around the house. When he did go to work he always made arrangements with Granny Gailbraith to stay with Ella.

Everything might have turned out all right, except for the storm. It blew in from the north one quiet June afternoon and by sundown the rain was beating the corn into the ground and Village Creek was overrunning its banks. Big flashes of lightning were streaking the sky and the thunder was so loud it seemed to come right into the room with you.

That was the night Ella's baby was born. The first Granny Gailbraith knew about it, Jim was pounding on her door and shouting above the storm. She opened the door and he stumbled into the room, drenched to the skin and wild-eyed with fright and grief.

"Go to Ella," he said. "I'm goin' after Doc Harris."

Granny went to fetch Jim a coat, but when she came back he had run out into that mad night, on his

way to town. Granny closed her house and started up
the road to Ella. It wasn't easy going even for an able-
bodied man, and Granny was old. The road was heavy
with mud and Granny could hardly walk. She said later
that she started to give up after she had gone half way
but knowing that Ella needed her kept her going. The
rain almost blinded her and the lightning and thunder
kept her awesome company.

Granny may not have had much strength, but she
had heart; and she finally managed to struggle up to
Ella's house. What she found kept her from resting even
for a minute. Granny went to work helping Ella, hoping and praying at first that the doctor and Jim would
arrive before long. Then the long hours became a nightmare of misery and grief. While the lightning flashed
and the thunder rolled down the valley, Granny tried to
help Ella fight her battle. They didn't have much
chance. Maybe even Doc Harris couldn't have helped.
But, of course, nobody could ever be sure about that,
because Doc Harris never arrived.

Finally, though, the storm was over and so was
Ella's ordeal. She sank into a long sleep and when she
awoke her parlor was filled with neighbors, talking in
hushed tones. But Granny Gailbraith was sitting by
her bed and Ella smiled and asked: "My baby . . . ?"

Tears came to Granny's eyes, but she stroked Ella's
hand and whispered, "Your baby is gone, child. He
was a fine, strong boy, but I couldn't make him breathe."

A shadow flickered across Ella's eyes and her chin
quivered but she didn't cry. She asked Granny, "And
Jim . . . ? Tell Jim I want to see him."

Granny was crying openly now. But all she could do was hold Ella's hand and tell her the truth. "Jim and his son are together, child."

Ella was never right after that. She didn't cry. She just lay there in bed, stunned. There was a far-away look in her eyes. After a day, she suddenly laughed. Then again and again. She laughed for two days and the sound made the neighbors hold their ears. People doubted if she ever knew that they had found Jim's body in Village Creek, that, half-blinded by rain, he had plunged into the rushing waters when North Bridge had suddenly been swept away while he was crossing it. If Ella ever knew that she didn't mention it. She never repeated Jim's name again. She just lay in bed and looked into space.

After a while she was able to get up. The first thing she did was to go to that buggy and croon and cluck to the baby which nobody but herself could see. At first, people thought she would get over it. They humored her because they realized that it would be better for her to escape her grief than it would be for her to face it.

But somehow Ella never did get around to facing the truth, and after we used to leave her pushing her empty buggy, Grandpa would say: "It's a shame so much motherhood has to be goin' to waste."

I thought I knew what Grandpa meant and it wasn't until Amos Smith's wife died that I realized I didn't. Amos, you might say, was the most shiftless man in Walesburg, but it wasn't altogether his fault. The fact that he was a clay-eater proved that. It proved that Amos never had a chance. Clay-eaters are like people from another world. It wasn't just because they could could pick up a chunk of clay and eat it like an apple; they just looked different, all hollow-eyed and skinny and sort of yellow looking.

Grandpa said they started eating clay when they were little children. Mostly they were children who were always hungry, and when they played in the dirt, making mud pies, they would nibble a little. The very weight of the clay helped to fill their empty stomachs. Pretty soon, they actually learned to like the taste of clay, like a man learns to like tobacco or sugar whiskey. There weren't many clay-eaters around Walesburg but I learned to tell them all right off by their looks.

I knew Amos better than any of them. He lived in a shack down near the depot. His wife, Annie, was a washerwoman and right up to the day her baby was born she worked over her tubs. Two days later she was back at work again and lots of folks said that's what killed her. Anyway, she died and the whole town turned out for her funeral. After it was over, the women started worrying about what to do with her little baby.

Bill Mackay and his wife wanted the baby awfully bad but Iris Thomas said no. Miss Iris was an old maid and she had devoted her whole life to taking care of unfortunate people. She was a tall, prim woman with a thin mouth. Grandpa always said it was a shame she couldn't help the unfortunate without making them feel that way. Grandpa didn't dislike Miss Iris, but he used to chuckle and say that it was too bad that such a sweet rose had such long, sharp thorns.

We were eating supper one night when Grandpa asked: "Has Iris decided what to do with the Smith baby?"

"Why, yes, she has, and it's a wonderful idea," Grandma said. "You'll never guess." Grandma looked awfully pleased and beaming about it.

"I hoped she'd let Bill and Helen Mackay have the boy," Grandpa said.

Grandma beamed some more, and then she was so pleased, she just couldn't keep the news any longer. She blurted right out: "Iris has decided to give the poor baby to Ella Wiley."

I was so pleased I wiggled my toes, but Grandpa got so red in the face he almost choked on a mouthful of corn bread. "Ella Wiley? Ella Wiley!" he said, sitting up very stiff. "Has Iris Thomas lost her mind?"

"Don't you think Ella can care for a baby?" Grandma said, raising her eyebrows.

"Of course, Ella can care for a baby," Grandpa said. Then he added quietly, "But Ella has a baby."

Grandma and I were so surprised I guess our mouths fell open. Then Grandma spoke right up. "Mr. Gray, I don't think you should joke about . . ."

Grandpa didn't seem to be listening. He was just staring across the table. "Ella has a baby," he said, "and I aim to see that nobody takes it away from her." Then he looked at Grandma: "When is Iris planning to make these arrangements?"

"Tomorrow at Ladies' Aid Meeting," Grandma said.

"I'll be there," Grandpa said.

"Well, I'll never . . ." Grandma began, but Grandpa said: "Pass the okra, please."

Grandma started to say something else, but she closed her mouth real tight and passed Grandpa the okra. It was easy to see she wasn't pleased at all.

When Grandpa had taken a helping of okra, he passed the bowl back to Grandma and smiled at her across the table. When she didn't smile back, he sort of grinned and lowered his head and cleared his throat: "Hrrmmph!"

VIII

I ALWAYS knew when it was Grandma's day to have Ladies' Aid. She was up almost as early as Old Gabriel, our rooster, and she made nearly as much noise. I could hear her from 'way up in my room, dusting off everything two or three times, and scurrying back and forth to the kitchen to see how her chocolate cake was coming.

Grandpa always acted as if he was surprised by all the bustle, even if he had seen it repeated over and over again for forty years. He would deliberately take his time at breakfast just to tease Grandma. She finally would get so impatient that she would begin to take the dishes off the table while he had a second helping of grits. Grandpa would raise his eyebrows like he was surprised. "Am I too pokey this mornin'?"

"Mister Gray," Grandma would say, "you *know* I have company comin' in today."

Grandpa would raise his eyebrows higher. "Who's comin'," he would say, "the King of Siam?"

Grandma's lips would get tight like they always did when Grandpa teased. "Mister Gray, I'm havin' Ladies' Aid today."

"Well, well," Grandpa would say, "that should be a very interestin' meetin'."

Then, while Grandma turned and went into the kitchen he would lower his head and grin at me across the table. "Ladies' Aid, son, beats spring cleanin' all hollow."

Men weren't generally allowed to attend Ladies' Aid, though sometimes they had men speakers. Once they even had a missionary who had been teaching the heathens in China and Africa.

He was a tall, gaunt man with deep-set eyes. I remembered him mostly because he shook a bony finger under my nose because he thought I didn't bow my head enough when Grandpa said grace at dinner. I would have felt real bad about it, except that I saw a sly look in Grandpa's eyes and I knew he didn't care.

"Always bow your head in deep humility when you are about to receive God's bountiful blessings," the missionary said. I bobbed my head because I couldn't think of anything to say. I was that surprised. That must have been all right because the missionary turned his attention to Grandma's fried chicken. We sat wide-eyed at his appetite. I thought he would never get enough. Later Grandpa chuckled and said the missionary was the

58

only man he ever saw who had eyes to match his stomach.

"What do you mean?" Grandma asked.

"Hollow!" said Grandpa.

"Why, Mister Gray," Grandma said, like she was shocked. But she grinned.

That missionary was a sort of joke at our table after that. Ever so often Grandpa would look up after grace and say, "I never could understan' how that missionary fellow *knew* son didn't bow his head—or how he got a drumstick in his hand soon's I said Amen."

My favorite of all the speakers who spoke before Ladies' Aid was Dr. Amos Britt. Dr. Britt wasn't a real doctor. Grandpa said he got that title because he went to school a long time and learned about books like Young Doc Harris learned about bodies.

Dr. Britt was a little wisp of a man with a neatly-trimmed spade beard. He could recite almost any poem anyone named. He recited Robert Burns' poems with a Scottish burr and he knew a lot of love poems that made all the women dab at their eyes with handkerchiefs.

I was awfully sorry when Ladies' Aid decided not to have Dr. Britt anymore. But, of course, they couldn't afford to have him come back after the day he spent three hours in Jere Higham's while waiting for his train. Lots of the ladies saw Jere put him aboard the 5:10. The doctor was hollering he was Lochinvar out of the West.

Most always I knew what went on at Ladies' Aid meeting when it met with Grandma. I would climb into the big fig tree outside our parlor window and sit there quietly, hearing everything. Sometimes the meetings were so dull that I wouldn't stay more than a few minutes. At other times I would crowd close to the window.

On the day that Ladies' Aid met to decide what to do with the Smith baby I climbed the fig tree early. I could hear Iris Thomas' high-pitched voice, asking for reports from the welfare and financial committees. Then the ladies sang a couple of hymns. About half-way through the second one, I knew that Grandpa had come in. All the ladies missed a note or two and then they started singing louder. Grandpa always said that folks worshiped just a little harder when a preacher was looking at them.

After the hymn, Gussie Lou Liles read a paper on Walt Whitman and Mrs. Sam Parsons told about plans for the annual box supper.

Then I heard Iris Thomas' voice again. "It is an unexpected pleasure to have Parson Gray with us today. All of us wish to say welcome, Parson. We'd be happy if you would favor us with a few words."

All the ladies clapped and I knew Grandpa was getting to his feet. He cleared his throat. "It's always a fine thing to see so many public-spirited ladies—an' so many lovely ones," he said. There were a lot of giggles at this. Grandpa went on, "I like to drop in on Ladies' Aid every chance I get. Somehow I always leave feelin' a little better, feelin' a little prouder of our town. Now I want you ladies to go right ahead with your meetin'. Don't let me get in the way."

The ladies clapped some more and I could hear the rustle of their dresses as they settled back in their chairs. Iris Thomas thanked Grandpa and then her voice got more businesslike. "Ladies," she said, "you all know of the tragedy that has visited our town. We are faced with the sad task of placing a poor, homeless child. This unfortunate child, a little boy, is at present being cared for by Mr. and Mrs. William Mackay. Now both Bill and Helen want to keep this child . . ." There was a sprinkling of applause, but Iris kept on talking and it died out.

"Now we know," she said, "that Bill and Helen would make fine parents. Ordinarily, we would feel that any unfortunate child would be lucky to have such a fine home." She paused a moment. "But, ladies, I have made a careful investigation—as I usually do in such cases—and I believe that you'll agree with me that someone else should get this Smith child." There was a lot of whispering at this, and I heard Granny Gailbraith's cracked voice:

"Just who do you have in mind, Iris?"

Iris' voice was almost breathless with triumph. "I believe," she said, "that we should give this child to another person in the community—a person who has suffered a great sorrow. This person would make an ideal mother. I think you'll agree." There was more excited whispering. I could tell the ladies were almost beside themselves with curiosity. Iris let that curiosity ripple over the crowd for a few moments before she spoke. I knew her eyes were bright and her cheeks were flushed. She was that proud.

"I mean," she said, "—I mean a poor unfortunate sister—Ella Wiley!"

Every woman in that room seemed to gasp. Then

they started clapping their hands and chattering excitedly. They all thought it was a wonderful idea. I could just see Iris Thomas standing there, feeling proud as punch and looking superior.

Then she spoke up again. "Ladies . . . ladies," she said, "I believe Parson Gray wants to say a word."

Grandpa's voice sounded almost happy, and I nearly fell out of the fig tree from surprise. "You know," he said, "I don't know what this town would do without Iris Thomas. Whenever tragedy or disaster falls, as it must do, ladies, she's always there to help out. Yes, I think we owe Iris Thomas a risin' vote of thanks. I'll get around to puttin' that in the form of a motion in a few minutes." There was some more clapping and whispering.

"You ladies know," Grandpa went on, "that nothin' is dearer to a mother than a baby. Our hearts have gone out to Sister Wiley for years. Many's the time I have seen Sister Wiley and thought to myself just how unfortunate it is that all her mother's love is being lavished on an empty buggy. It's enough to bring the tears to your eyes." He raised his voice questioningly: "I suppose Sister Wiley is very pleased with your plan, Iris?"

"Why . . . why, I haven't mentioned it to her yet, Parson," Iris said. Then she sort of laughed. "But of course we all know how very pleased she will be. It does my heart good to think how happy poor Ella will be."

"Yes indeed," Grandpa said, "an' well she might. It's a fine thing you are doin'." He lowered his voice a little. "I was just sort of wonderin' what Ella will do with that child she thinks she has now." He laughed, like the whole thing was ridiculous.

"Of course," Grandpa said, "we know that Ella doesn't have a baby, but I think you'll all agree that the only thing peculiar about Ella's mother love is that she's carried it too far." Grandpa chuckled. "All mothers are guilty of that, more or less, I reckon. Did you ever see a mother who thought her child was ugly? 'Course you never did. He can have squint eyes and jug-handle ears, but his face is a beautiful sight to his mother."

There was a lot of giggling. Grandpa waited until it stopped.

"An' did you ever see a mother who thought her son was bad?" he went on. " 'Course you never did! When the James boys were shootin' up trains an' robbin' banks their mamma thought they were jest misunderstood." Grandpa paused a moment and I knew he was smiling and nodding his head. Then his voice was lower. "Yes, mothers are jest blind. Sometimes they jest can't see like other folks. Sometimes I think about that when I look at Ella. She's been seein' a perfect little baby for years." His voice was earnest. "That baby's real to her. An' another thing—Ella has been carryin' a heavier load than most mothers. She hasn't jest had to correct her child's looks or character. Ella's had to create a baby. That baby is in her carriage, that pitiful, wornout carriage. It would be wonderful if she had a real baby in there. That would be a happy endin' to her story."

Grandpa paused a long time and when he continued his voice sounded soft and wistful, like it did sometimes

63

when he prayed in church. "It would certainly be wonderful," he said, "if we could always write happy endin's to stories." He sighed. "But we can't do that, ladies—no, we can't—'specially when we deal with true-to-life, livin' stories. Only the people who are carryin' the burdens can set them down—only the people who are makin' the stories can write the endin's. Ella wrote her's. She lost her baby, so she found one anyway. Ella lost her baby once. If you put another child in that carriage she will lose it twice."

There was a long silence. I didn't know Grandpa had sat down until someone coughed and broke the spell. There was the rustle of dresses as the women stirred a little. Then there was another awkward silence. Nobody seemed to know what to say. Finally Iris Thomas spoke up. Her voice was high-pitched. "Parson Gray's point is well made, I'm sure—but—er, ah, I think we should have some more discussion." She hesitated a second. "What do you think, Miz Cameron?"

I might have known Iris would call on Thelma Cameron. She was a stout woman with a jutting chin. Next to Iris she took more interest in welfare matters than anyone in town. I'd heard some folks whisper that she could have spent more time with her own three skinny little girls, but maybe that was just gossip. The only time I'd ever heard Grandpa mention Mrs. Cameron was one day when he scandalized Grandma. He said that when he saw Mrs. Cameron walk down Main Street it reminded him of a ship being launched.

It was plain that Mrs. Cameron didn't know what to do at first. She got to her feet and coughed and cleared her throat a lot. Finally she must have decided she'd best agree with Iris.

"I just don't know whether I agree with Parson Gray," she said in her proper voice. "Of course, I'm a woman—" and here she gave a little laugh—"and I guess I do like to see happy endings. Maybe that's wrong, but I've never thought so. I don't think any of us know too much about human minds. Ella Wiley may think she has a baby all right, but I think it's high time we quit humoring her."

She hesitated a moment. "After all, Ella Wiley *doesn't* have a baby. For my part I've never asked about the child she thinks she has. I've always believed that, sooner or later, someone should get around to making her face the fact that she's being ridiculous. If it's a baby that Ella wants—well, now I think we're in a position to make her forget this nonsense!" Mrs. Cameron sat down heavily. There was deep silence.

For a moment I thought that had settled it. Whenever Iris Thomas and Mrs. Cameron teamed up they usually had their way. Then I heard Grandpa's voice again. "One more thing, Iris," he said, and I knew he had gotten to his feet. "For mah part, I think Miz Cameron has a mighty convincin' argument. She may be right—but I'd like to ask a question for mah own satisfaction. How many ladies present have children?"

There was a bustle and I knew almost every woman in that room had raised her hand, except maybe Iris Thomas. There was a smile in Grandpa's voice. "That's an awful lot o' motherhood," he said. A little ripple of laughter swept the room.

"Now," said Grandpa, and his voice was soft, "how many mothers here have lost children?"

There was more stirring. I knew a good many hands had gone up.

Grandpa's voice was still soft. "Thank you," he said. "I know you mothers must know how Ella feels. You've lost children—but yet they've never gone either. You hold them as close and as dear as you do the ones playin' around your knee. You see, you have memories of them. An' those memories you carry in your minds and in your hearts. No—those children aren't gone. When you pause sometimes can't you see them—can't you almost hear them? Yes, there are some things that never disappear, an' a mother's love for a child is one of them.

"There's not as much difference between Ella and us as you might think. I've lost a son an' I still hold him close in my heart. You do the same thing. But Ella? Well, Ella goes further than we do. She doesn't carry her memories hidden inside her. Ella couldn't stan' that. No—Ella carries her lost child in a buggy. Ella talks to her child. 'Course she does. So do you."

Grandpa paused for a moment and when he started talking again it was almost as if he was thinking out loud. "Ella couldn't face reality. Now we want to wake her up. I don't think we'd best do that. If she had been the sort of person who could have faced the truth, she would have done so. I think that what we should do when we look in Ella's buggy is to try to see it through her eyes. There's no baby there—yes, we know that. But, ladies, remember this—no one else can see your memories. Does that mean they don't exist? You know the answer. Ella's baby is as real as our memories."

There was a long silence. I sat holding to the trunk of that fig tree and thinking. For the first time I guess I saw Ella as she really was. Then I remembered one time when I was in the parlor alone. I looked up at my mother's picture and for a moment she seemed awfully close. Almost without realizing it, I whispered, "Mama, I hope you're happy." It didn't seem at all odd.

I thought about that a moment and then I realized someone else was talking at the meeting. I leaned closer to the window. It was Granny Gailbraith. She must have been standing because her old voice was slow and breathless. "Yes," she said, "I know what the parson means. I've lost five children—five o' the nine children I brought into this world.

"The Lord took them and I didn't question Him." Granny sighed and her voice seemed to get stronger. "There is one thing I know—and I suppose it sounds funny. When I think of my lost children I don't think of them being grown men and women at all. I remember them as babies. I remember them as they were sleeping so sound or gurgling so gentle in their cradles.

"Sometimes I've even thought that Ella Wiley has been lucky. That's strange, I reckon, but I keep thinking that Ella will never lose her child. Most mothers do. Children grow up. I cried when they went off to school. And do you remember how it hurts to have them grow up?" Granny sighed again. "Those are foolish sorrows, I know—but I did have them. Ella can't

67

lose her baby. She'll always have it. If it makes her happy I want her to keep it."

After Granny sat down there was an awkward pause again, and then Iris spoke. There was an edge to her voice and I knew she didn't like the way things were going at all. "Well . . . I . . . I think . . ." she began, but Granny Gailbraith cut in.

"I make a motion that we give the Smith baby to Bill and Helen Mackay," she said.

Iris hesitated for a long time. "Do I hear a second to this motion?" she almost snapped.

Every woman in the room seemed to speak up. Iris didn't have any choice. "All in favor will raise their right hands."

I knew what had happened by the way Iris rapped her gavel. Her voice was shrill. "Meeting's adjourned for refreshments."

I shinnied down out of the fig tree and ran around to the back door. Grandpa was standing at the kitchen table, licking the icing off a piece of Grandma's chocolate cake. I could hear the buzz of the ladies' voices in the parlor.

When Grandpa saw me he looked out of the corner of his eye and grinned. I grinned back.

"Grandpa," I said, "is . . . is it true that mothers see their children different—is it, Grandpa?"

Grandpa's grin got broader. " 'Course it is, son— sure as I'm sittin' heah, right this minute—I'd swear you didn't have a single freckle." He cut me a piece of cake and we sat down, grinning, and ate. My grandpa and I understood each other.

68

IX

NOBODY in Walesburg had less than Chloroform Wiggins, and nobody felt better. Grandpa always said that he knew a lot of men who were looking for contentment, and he knew a few who had found it, but Chloroform Wiggins was the first man he had ever seen who was born with it.

At that, it wasn't much of a surprise. Chloroform came from a long line of contented folks. His father, Sam, and his mother, Aggie, were river people. For well on to thirty years they floated up and down the Black Warrior. They seldom put a foot ashore, except to buy some fatback or salt, or maybe fresh vegetables when they were in season. They didn't always even have to do this.

That was because Sam and Aggie had the strangest

boat anyone had ever seen. It was a big, flat-bottomed barge and it looked like a floating island. Sam had scooped up some rich bottom land and stacked it deep and rich all over one corner of the barge. This was his garden and he grew tomatoes and okra and onions and salad greens just like anybody else. In another corner of his barge, Sam had a little pen. In this he used to keep four or five chickens and maybe a duck or two. In still another corner, Sam had a stronger pen and it usually hemmed up an old sow, with sometimes even a litter of pigs.

Right in the center of all this, Sam had built a little four-room house, as compact and as neat as could be.

People used to call Sam and Aggie's home the Ark. It was really quite a sight. Everybody on the river learned to know it—and also Sam and Aggie. That was a good thing. When Sam wanted to go downstream, he just cast off a line and away he went. But getting back upstream, of course, was quite a trick. Sam had to depend on the good nature of river-boat captains. They seldom let him down. He would stand in the corner of the Ark, holding up a line and hollering, and usually it wasn't long before some boat saw him and heaved to. Sam would throw his towline to the grinning crew and they would make it fast. Then up the river they would go, with the river boat puffing and snorting under the double load.

Sam and Aggie got along fine on that old boat for twenty years. Then one day, to their surprise, they discovered that they were going to need a doctor. And that was one thing the Ark didn't have.

The very thought of having a baby scared Sam and Aggie almost as much as it pleased them, though, and they decided to stay put until it was born. They tied up at Boyd's Landing. Sam even got a part-time job at the cotton gin to earn enough money to pay Old Doc Harris.

Professionally speaking, Old Doc wasn't too pleased about the Wiggins' baby. Aggie wasn't getting any younger and he just couldn't make any promises about how things would turn out. He tried to hide his worry by joshing Aggie.

"Aggie," he said, "why did you and Sam wait all these years to start a crop o' chil'lun?"

Aggie grinned shyly. "Shecks, Doc Harris, we'uns didn't wait—the Lawd did."

At that Old Doc shook his head and smiled dryly. "Aggie, I jest hope the Lawd keeps on takin' a special interest in your case."

Old Doc didn't say so, but he knew that when Aggie's baby started on the way it wasn't going to be so much a question of him helping the Lord as it was of the Lord helping him. And that was the way it was. When Sam, all red-faced and excited, came running one day to fetch him, Old Doc packed his little black bag and took his time about getting down to the Ark. When he got there, he took a seat in a big rocker and just waited. He waited a long time, and about all he could do was to get up every one in a while and wet a towel from a bottle and take it over to the bed where Aggie lay tight-jawed and white faced.

"Heah, breathe deep, Aggie," he would say. Aggie

would take big, grateful breaths and some of the strain would go out of her face.

Every time she would whisper, "Thankee, Doc."

That went on for a long time, and, then, finally Aggie's baby was born. It was a boy. Sam was almost beside himself.

Before Old Doc Harris left, he walked over to the bed to take a last look at Aggie. She looked up, all misty-eyed and happy. "Ah . . . Ah bin meanin' to ast," she said, "—Ah want to know—what was that sweet-smellin' stuff you give me?"

"Why, that was chloroform," Old Doc said.

Aggie said the word a couple of times, "Chloroform . . . chloroform—that's mighty purty." Then she was fast asleep.

When she awakened Sam was sitting by the bed. She grinned at him a little weakly. Then she asked shyly, "Sam, have you got your mind set on havin' our young'un named after you?"

" 'Course not," Sam said.

Aggie hesitated a minute. "Then, Sam, eff'n you don't mind, could we name him Chloroform? Hit's a medicine name, Sam. Hit's the purtiest name Ah ever heered."

That was the way Chloroform got his name, and he was always happy with it. He grew up on the Ark and he liked it so much that he almost never put a foot ashore. Then, when he was a skinny, tow-headed boy of sixteen, Sam died. He and Aggie buried Sam in the river and then they started drifting again—just the two of them.

Somehow things were never the same after that, though. Within two years Aggie died. Chloroform tried living alone for about a year, but the nights were long and lonely and the days were dull. The Ark began to fall to pieces. One day a barge captain offered Chloroform a hundred dollars for the Ark and he took it. He packed up a few odds and ends in an old straw valise and came to Walesburg to see Old Doc Harris.

Old Doc took some of the money and bought Chloroform twenty acres of land out near Brown's Spring. With the rest of the money he hired a couple of men to help Chloroform build a little house. Then right away people found out that while Chloroform had left the river—the river had never left Chloroform. He wanted his house to be the same size as the one on the Ark. Old Doc Harris and the men argued with him, but he just flatly refused to have his house any bigger. Finally they gave up, and it was built the way he wanted it.

But that wasn't all. Chloroform had twenty acres, but he never used more than a half acre of it. He put up pens for chickens and pigs at the corners of his little shack. Right near the back door he started a tiny garden. Chloroform just forgot about the rest of his land. All he was interested in was that little plot which wasn't much bigger than the Ark.

Folks laughed about Chloroform, but they had to admit that he never bothered anybody. When he needed something he didn't have, he offered to work to earn it. But Chloroform never seemed to want much. He was just plain satisfied and nobody had ever been able to make him any other way. A lot of men tried it

73

one day down at Clem McCollough's store, and Grandpa used to chuckle and say that probably it was the hardest test any mortal man had withstood.

It was a rainy afternoon and the men were standing around because there didn't seem much else to do. They all looked up and grinned when Chloroform came in, and I guess they had reason. Chloroform was quite a sight. He had cut a hole in a big square of wagon canvas, and had thrust his head through it like it was a poncho. It completely covered his scrawny little frame. Not even his feet showed. Rain had plastered Chloroform's straw-colored hair down flat, except for a cowlick in back which stood up like an Indian's feather. He had a long, thin neck with a big adam's apple, and, as usual, his pointed face was covered with a big grin. Chloroform stood in the doorway a minute with the water pouring down off his poncho and making big puddles at his feet. He shook himself a few times and then he looked up and his grin got broader.

"Rainin' like thunder," he said.

Perry Lokey was sitting on a box near the door, and he looked up like he was surprised. "Naw," he said.

Chloroform looked at his solemn face, and his grin flickered out. He looked at the other men, but they had surprised looks on their faces, too. He stood there a second and then he carefully rubbed his hand over his head and then looked at it to be sure it was wet. He turned and went to the door and looked out. When he turned around again his grin was as big as ever. "Yep, John," he said. "Hit's sho rainin'. Reckon you bin asleep."

The other men almost choked over this, but they didn't let on. They winked and looked wise.

Chloroform didn't seem to notice. He walked over to Old Man McCollough behind the counter.

"Clem," he said, "Ah aim to try to git a mess o' cats down in the creek after this downpour stops. Ah'll be happy to bring you some, eff'n you kin see your way clear to let me have a number-four hook. Ah ain't got no hooks big enough for cats. Don't know eff'n you think hits a fair swap or not, but Ah'll be plumb grateful eff'n you can oblige."

Old Man McCollough smiled. "Why, sure, Chloroform, it's mor'n fair. I could use a mess of cats." He turned to get the hooks when Perry Lokey spoke up.

"Do you think *one* hook is enough, Chloroform?"

Chloroform looked sort of surprised. "Why, Ah reckon hit is, Perry. Ah ain't gonna put out a trotline, Ah jest aim to stillfish."

Perry got up and came over to Chloroform, and the crowd in the store sniggered and winked.

Perry put his hand on Chloroform's shoulder. "Now I don't want you to think I'm tryin' to mind your business," he said, "but I think you ought to take along another hook—jest in case."

Chloroform blinked. "Jest in case o' what, Perry?"

Perry was looking downright serious. "Well, jest in case that hook gets caught on a log—or maybe even a big ole cat too heavy for you to land comes along and breaks it off your line. How 'bout your line, Chloroform? Is it strong? Don't you think you'd better take along a new line, too."

75

"Wal, Ah don't . . ."

"Now don't be too hasty, Chloroform," Perry said. "Think this over. Suppose a big ole cat does break that line. Suppose he steals your hook. What you goin' to do then?"

Chloroform opened his mouth a couple of times like he was going to say something, but the words didn't seem to come.

Perry went on. "Chloroform, the trouble with you is that you don't worry none. That's downright sinful these days. Everybody's got to worry."

Chloroform looked around slowly to see if anybody was laughing. Not a face cracked in that store. When he spoke he sounded almost ashamed. "But . . . but, Perry, Ah jest ain't got nothin' to worry about."

Everybody laughed at this, and when he heard them, Chloroform seemed to feel a little better. He started grinning again, but he stopped when he looked at Perry and saw his face was still solemn.

Perry shook his head sorrowfully. "Chloroform, you aren't doin' right by this heah community. You aren't pullin' your load. You're a-lettin' your neighbors worry for you." He pointed his finger at Chloroform. "You ought to be ashamed of yourself!"

That startled Chloroform so much that his mouth fell open. He didn't know what to say.

Perry pointed his finger at him again. "I worry," he said. "Clem McCollough worries, an' everybody in this heah store worries 'cept you. Now what are you goin' to do about it?"

Chloroform just shook his head and gulped.

76

Perry made a clucking sound of pity. He shook his head slowly. "Chloroform, you got to take on some responsibility. It's downright shameful the way you take everythin' so soft and easy." He lowered his head and put his hand over his mouth like he was pondering, but it was hiding a big grin.

Then Perry looked up quickly and snapped his fingers. "I got it, Chloroform—you've got to get in debt. What do you want more than anything right this minute?"

Chloroform's eyes were wide now. He swallowed a couple of times and wet his lips with his tongue. "Why, nothin', Perry, 'ceptin' a number-four hook, Ah reckon."

Perry snorted. "That doesn't amount to a thing." He looked around at the men in the store and winked. "Does it, men?" They all shook their heads.

"Now, lookit, Chloroform," Perry said, "you look around this store and pick out something you want. Me and the boys will buy it for you. Then you'll be in debt to us." He raised his finger and shook it at Chloroform. "Then you'll have to worry about payin' us back."

Chloroform had a hard time finding his voice, "Shecks, Perry . . ."

Perry waved his protest aside. "Go ahead and look," he said. "You've got to pull your share of the load in this heah community."

Chloroform sort of sighed and then he started looking all around in that big old store. He looked at the horse collars and rat traps hanging from the ceiling. He looked at all the cases with thread and candy and tape measures. He looked at all the bins with beans and crackers and dried fruits. He looked at hoes and rakes and plows. He even looked at the racks where Clem McCollough had hung calico and taffeta dresses. It took a long time, and finally when he turned back to look at Perry his face was red and embarrassed.

He sort of stammered. "Ah . . . Ah reckon Ah jest don't want a thing—'ceptin' a number-four hook."

Everybody roared at this, and even Perry had a hard time keeping his face straight. "All right, Chloroform," he said, "Clem McCollough's stock jest isn't big enough for you. We got to get a bigger selection." He turned to Clem McCollough. "Clem, pass over that Sears, Roebuck catalog." He took the big book and handed it to Chloroform. "Sit down over there on that cracker barrel and pick out something you want."

Chloroform took the catalog and sat down. Everybody watched his face as he turned the pages. It took a long time. He looked at Congress gaiters and long flannels. He looked at windmills and tin bath tubs. He even looked at fancy cowboy boots and slick buggies. He lingered a while over fine fishing tackle and double-barreled shotguns. He looked at everything that is aimed to make a man's life brighter and easier. Finally he turned the last page, and looked up at the men in the store.

They weren't grinning or sniggering now. They were just waiting. "Well, Chloroform," Perry asked, "what do you want?"

Chloroform's face got beet-red. He licked his lips and it was plain to see that he was floundering with embarrassment. His voice was low. "Ah . . . Ah . . . reckon—that is—well, Ah reckon Ah don't want anythin' 'ceptin' a number-four hook." He looked at the silent men and tried to grin. "Everything's mighty purty, though."

Clem McCollough spoke quietly. "Heah's yore hook, Chloroform."

"Thankee, Clem," Chloroform said. He hunched the poncho up about his shoulders and turned and told Perry Lokey and the others good bye. The men watched him go silently, with respect in their eyes.

There was a long silence, and then the men began to shuffle their feet uncomfortably and clear their throats. Perry Lokey tried to force a laugh.

"It beats the life outta me," he said. "He don't want nothin'. Reckon there's never been anybody like that before."

Clem McCollough's eyes were thoughtful. He shook his head slowly. His voice was low. "Yes, thar has," he said. "Ah heard of somebody else like that. They didn't have catalogs in those days, so they let Him look around from a mountain top."

Clem smiled. "He didn't want nothin' yo' could carry in yore hands or put in yore pocket." Then Clem did a funny thing. He looked around that big old store of his, and his eyes swept the overflowing shelves and the bulging bins and the full racks. "Sometimes," he said, and his voice sounded like he was thinking out loud, "sometimes Ah think that Ah'm a mighty pore man."

X

GRANDPA used to say that Young Doc Harris was the most successful failure he knew. That sounded odd, but Young Doc was an odd man. In the first place, he wasn't very young at all. He was about thirty-five. Folks called him Young Doc because they had called his father Old Doc. Almost everybody in Walesburg still remembered Old Doc, though ivy almost covered his grave out at Rehobeth Cemetery.

Young Doc wasn't a bit like his father had been. Old Doc was a big, jovial man with a tobacco-stained mustache. His clothes were as wrinkled as a scarecrow's. Young Doc was tall and his stiff black hair was close-clipped. His voice was precise. Maybe he would have been handsome, except that his face was stern. He almost never smiled. He was as clean as a fresh-peeled buckeye.

Old Doc used to laugh and say that he learned medicine by holding a doctor's horse and sweeping out his office. Maybe that's why he saw to it that Young Doc got so much education. Nobody could deny that it was considerable. Young Doc graduated from Tulane Medical School down in New Orleans. After that he went off to a foreign school in Vienna. I guess Young Doc learned everything there was to know about medicine, but he didn't seem to know much about people. He would sit at a man's bedside for two days, curing him of an ailment, but when he passed him on the street later, he would barely nod.

Maybe all of Young Doc's education was responsible for so few folks understanding him. Lots of folks didn't even try. They hollered for Young Doc when they were sick, but they left him alone when they were well and feeling good.

That didn't bother Young Doc at all. The plain fact was that he always had the notion that he didn't belong in our town. At the same time, he knew that the town couldn't get along without him. That's what Grandpa meant when he said Young Doc was a successful failure.

Folks who remembered said that when Young Doc was a boy he wasn't any different from anyone else. But it was natural, I guess, that all that education was bound to make a difference. Grandpa said he noticed it right off when Young Doc came back from Vienna.

Old Doc was getting pretty feeble then, but he was as happy as a kid. He started taking Young Doc around with him on all his calls and he almost keeled over with surprise when he saw how Young Doc knew his business. He got put out with him occasionally, too, especially when Young Doc made him wear a white gown and a piece of cloth across his face every time he operated or delivered a baby.

"Why, dadblamit, son," he would roar, "Ah've been bringin' babies into this world for fifty-odd years, an' Ah ain't never put on a Mother Hubbard to do it!"

Young Doc just looked at him quietly. "You've been lucky," he said, "and luck has no part in medicine."

Old Doc couldn't do anything about that except mutter and blow at his mustache. By and large, he accepted most of Young Doc's new ideas, though every once in a while he would get so provoked at the mask across his face while he was delivering a baby that he would tear it off and use it to mop his flushed, round face. When he did this Young Doc wouldn't say a word. He'd just pick up another mask and hand it to his father. At first, Old Doc would bellow at this. Later he got to where he would just make a half-hearted protest, just sort of open and close his mouth but not making any sound. Finally, he got to carry gowns and masks even when Young Doc wasn't along, and he got to making quite a show when he put them on.

"Yes, sir," he would say, squaring his big shoulders into a white jacket, "this is the latest thing in antiseptic pree-cautions, an' there ain't anythin' too good for my patients. Nawsir, nothin'!"

Pretty soon Old Doc had picked up nearly all of Young Doc's tricks. He used to make jokes about it. "Why, dadblamit," he would tell the folks down at Clem McCollough's store, "that son o' mine is goin' to make a good doctor outta me yet." Old Doc would laugh then, and so would everybody else. They all knew there wasn't a better doctor anywhere than Old Doc Harris, even if he did drop pot likker on his vest and get tobacco juice in his mustache.

Every once in a while, though, Young Doc would get too modern and Old Doc would balk like a stubborn mule. One big thing they disagreed on was mad-dog bites. The first time it happened was when a mad fice dog bit Jim Bishop's little boy.

It was a pretty bad wound on the calf of the leg, all red and blue marked. The minute he saw it, Old Doc started heating an iron. Young Doc, though, turned to his satchel and started taking out a needle and he hollered for Black Jim to go down to the ice-house and get some medicine he had there.

Old Doc just stopped still. "What you plannin' on, son?" he asked.

"Why, I'm going to give him the Pasteur anti-rabies toxin," Young Doc said, sort of surprised.

"You mean you plan on givin' this chile shots for a dog bite?" Old Doc asked, flabbergasted.

"Certainly," Young Doc said.

Old Doc flushed in the face and his mouth opened and closed like a horsesucker's. He knew it wasn't any use arguing with Young Doc, though, and after a minute he quieted down and started heating his iron again.

"Son," he said, "Ah don't know about your method, but mine is sure-fire. You give him a needle, but Ah'll be dadblamed if you're goin' to keep me from cauterizin' that wound."

Young Doc let loose with one of his rare smiles at that. "All right, Papa," he said, "I'll cure him. You give him something to remember that dog by."

That was the way it was. Old Doc and Young Doc disagreed about some things, but everybody benefited by it. Then, one day, Old Doc had to stay at home and Young Doc made the calls alone. Old Doc started sinking fast after that and even Young Doc with all his foreign learning couldn't do anything for him. One windy night his tired heart stopped altogether. Young Doc carried on because he was Old Doc's bequest to the town. But somehow he never took his father's place.

Folks had loved and respected Old Doc. They just respected Young Doc, but that was all he asked, so I guess he was reasonably well satisfied.

One time I asked Grandpa about it. "Grandpa, Young Doc Harris isn't much like the other folks in Walesburg, is he?"

Grandpa sort of smiled. "Why, no, son, I reckon he isn't."

"He's awfully wise, though, isn't he, Grandpa?"

Grandpa sat still a moment, pondering that over. Then he answered slowly, like he was counting every word, "I wouldn't say that, son. Young Doc isn't too wise—but he is terribly smart."

I knew what Grandpa meant and I didn't say anything else. Grandpa and Young Doc never talked about

each other. It was sort of an agreement. Grandpa took
care of people's souls. Young Doc took care of their
bodies. They had tried to stay out of each other's ter-
ritory since one cold winter night shortly after Old
Doc died.

That was the night the Widow Helfin who ran the
boarding house down by the depot fell sick. People
thought a lot of the Widow Helfin because she had
spunk. When Sam Helfin died and left her and her four
children with nothing except a half-crib of corn, she
didn't go back home to her folks nor did she spend a lot
of time feeling sorry for herself. She turned her big old
yellow house into a rooming house. She never made
much money, but then, nobody ever had to take her
baskets on Christmas either. Her kids may not have
been the best dressed at school, but they were always
clean. The Widow Helfin had never bothered anybody, and she didn't when she got sick for the last time.
It was lightning pneumonia. Grandpa had no sooner
heard that the Widow Helfin was sick than word came
that she was dying. He went down to the boarding
house right away.

The house was all lit up because the neighbors had
come in, bringing extra lamps. They sat around in the
parlor whispering, like folks always do when death is
coming into a house. Cleedy Helfin met Grandpa at
the front door. "Ma's sinkin' fast," he said, with tears
in his eyes, "an' Ah want you to pray for her."

"That's what I'm heah for," Grandpa said. "Take
me to your ma."

It wasn't hard to find the Widow Helfin's room.

Her breathing was the loudest thing in that barny old house. Cleedy opened the door softly and Grandpa stepped into the room.

Young Doc Harris was sitting by the bed. He had been there for hours. His face was drawn with weariness and frustration, just like it always was when his medical skill and foreign learning couldn't beat back death. When he saw Grandpa he looked surprised, then his lips sort of twisted.

"What do you want?"

Grandpa looked him in the eye. "I've come to pray for Sister Helfin," he said.

Young Doc got up and his face was flushed. "I won't have you in here! I won't let this patient's family disturb her. I certainly won't let you bellow a prayer over her!"

Grandpa didn't say a word for a minute. He just stood there looking into Young Doc's drawn, angry face. Then he walked toward the bed where the Widow Helfin was tossing and tumbling.

"Easy, son, easy," he said. "I'm goin' to say a prayer—an' I'm goin' to say it now."

Young Doc just stood there stone-mad while Grandpa knelt by the bed and began to pray. Halfway through his prayer, the Widow Helfin quit tossing. Young Doc crossed to the bed and leaned over her. Grandpa kept on praying.

Finally he was through and he rose to his feet. He looked at the still figure on the bed and then at Young Doc.

"She's at peace now," Grandpa said.

Something like a sneer twisted Young Doc's face. "She's dead," he said, short-like. He pulled the sheet over the white face.

Grandpa looked at Young Doc and his face and voice were still calm. "That's what I mean—she has found peace at last."

Young Doc started to say something else, but Grandpa walked from the room and closed the door quietly after him.

After Grandpa had comforted the weeping Helfin children and made arrangements for their mother's burial, he left the house and walked into the cold night. He stood by the front steps a minute, breathing the frosty air and looking up at the stars. He gave a little start when he heard a noise behind him. He looked up and saw Young Doc standing on the veranda behind him.

"Snappish night, isn't it, Doctor?" Grandpa said.

Young Doc didn't answer. He walked down the steps and stood looking at Grandpa. "Mr. Gray," he said in his precise voice, "we must straighten out some things."

"Certainly," Grandpa said.

Grandpa's calmness made Young Doc so mad that his voice got tight. His breath came in little short bursts of white vapor. "Mr. Gray," he said, "as long as I'm the doctor in this town I don't intend to put up with your psalm-singing in sick rooms. I must demand that you confine your prayers to your church!"

Grandpa's voice was soft. "Son, if you want to see prayers confined to a church, you're practisin' in the wrong town. People come to church when their souls are calm. They pray when they need help."

Young Doc snorted. "I'm not interested in souls, Mr. Gray. I'm interested in curing people without interference. I've yet to see a soul."

For the first time Grandpa's voice was edged with cold. "I've heard that medical-student nonsense a lot o' times, Doctor, but never from a man as old—or who 'pears to be as sensible—as you are."

"When I go into a sick room, I'm in charge!" Young Doc snapped. "I want that understood."

Grandpa looked at his angry face for a full minute. He kept his voice soft. "No, you're not, son. You're not in charge—you're jest the foreman. You've got a boss and I've got a boss. We're jest in charge of different departments . . . like we were in there tonight. You do your job, an' I'll do mine. Someday you'll find out why we should help each other. I already know."

Grandpa turned and walked down the street. Young Doc stood there in that cold, starry night for a long time, alone with his thoughts, and just barely hearing the crying coming from the Helfin parlor. After a while he turned and walked away. He was still mad; but there was nothing he could do.

XI

GRANDPA and Young Doc saw each other in a lot of sick rooms after that but they never mentioned their differences. The nearest they ever came to it was when little Lennie Shelton got sick. When Grandpa arrived at the Shelton place, Bart Shelton was sitting on the veranda. He came out to the buggy and held old Joshua's head while Grandpa climbed down.

"How's that boy o' yours, Bart?" Grandpa asked.

Bart shook his head slowly. Grandpa could see that sleepless nights had deepened the lines in his face. "Porely, Parson," Bart said. "Jest porely."

They walked up to the veranda and sat there in the shade, talking about crops and their neighbors for a long time. Finally Grandpa pulled out his big old watch and looked at it. "Guess I'd best take a look at that boy an' be gettin' back to town," he said. Bart looked uncomfortable and squirmed a little. "Wal . . . I . . . I . . ."

Grandpa was surprised at first. But then he sighed and put his watch back in his pocket. "All right, Bart," he said, "what is it?"

Bart's face got red. "Wal, Parson, it's . . . it's Young Doc Harris. He tole me to keep everybody out of Lennie's room. Nobody can go in, 'cept Martha. I can't even go inside. I wanta go see that boy, but I can't."

Grandpa sat there looking across the fields for a minute. "You know, Bart," he said, "it's awfully hard to pick an argument with a doctor. Doctors are lucky that way. Anybody can argue with a preacher, an' most always they do. But a doctor—well, a doctor knows things we don't know. Every man thinks he knows his soul, but only a few know their bodies."

Grandpa stood up and there was a far-away look in his eyes. "Sometimes I wonder if people know why preachers come into homes where there is sickness." He turned to Bart. "Do you know, Bart?"

Bart shook his head slowly. "Why, I reckon . . . I reckon you're my friend, Parson."

Grandpa smiled. "That's true, Bart. I am your friend. But I'd be heah even if I wasn't. I have a duty, too, Bart. A man named Luke wrote it down. Jesus said it." Grandpa half closed his eyes and began to recite softly: "And into whatsoever city ye enter, and they receive you, eat such things as are set before you; and heal the sick that are therein, and say unto them,

'The kingdom of God is come nigh unto you.' But into whatsoever city ye enter, and they receive you not, go your ways out into the streets of the same, and say, 'Even the very dust of your city, which cleaveth on us, we do wipe off against you: notwithstanding be ye sure of this, that the kingdom of God is come nigh unto you.' But I say unto you, that it shall be more tolerable in that day for Sodom than for that city."

Then Grandpa put out his hand and said: "Good bye, Bart, I'll be goin' back to town."

Bart stood up slowly and his jaw was tight. "I'd be obliged if you'd wait a while, Parson. We'll go upstairs and say a prayer for that boy o' mine."

It was late afternoon when Grandpa headed back to town. When he reached the covered bridge, he heard the thump of another horse's hooves and he reined up to one side. It was Young Doc Harris. When he saw Grandpa he flushed and made to go on, but Grandpa stopped him. "Evenin', Doctor," he said, "could I have a word with you?"

Young Doc reined up and waited. He sat still and his eyes were cold. Grandpa didn't seem to notice.

"I've been out to Bart Shelton's," Grandpa said.

Young Doc didn't change expression. "Yes?" he said in his dry, precise voice.

"I thought I should tell you that I saw Bart's boy," Grandpa said.

Young Doc's face still didn't change, but his eyes seemed to get a little colder. "Mr. Gray," he said, "I suppose you know that I left orders that nobody was to enter that room except the boy's mother."

Grandpa nodded. "Yes, I knew. I stopped to tell you that I went anyway."

Young Doc twisted his lips into a half smile. "In that case, I suppose that you have taken over. I suppose that I can drive back to town, and leave the case in your learned hands."

Grandpa shook his head slowly. "No, son, that boy needs you."

Young Doc snorted. His voice was sarcastic. "More than religion?"

"No," said Grandpa. "Sick or well he needs religion. You'll make him well so he can enjoy it."

Young Doc's lips twisted again. "And suppose I refuse? Suppose I refuse because his family won't obey my orders. Why should I drive six miles a day to care for someone when it's evident that you can come along and countermand my orders?"

Grandpa's smile was kindly. "You'll go, son, because you're your father's son. You'll go because it's your duty." His voice was low. "You'll go because you have to do whatever you can—jest as I have to do what I can."

Young Doc looked at Grandpa for a long time. His eyes stayed cold and unyielding, but finally he clucked to his horse and drove on. Grandpa turned in his buggy and watched Young Doc's stiff back for a minute. Then he sighed and turned and flicked the reins. "Get along, Joshua."

That was the last time Grandpa saw Young Doc for a long time, but like everybody else he heard about Young Doc and Faith Samuels. Grandpa seemed pleased. He didn't even ask, like some folks did, what it was that a sweet woman like Faith could see in Young Doc. That was the way I felt.

Miss Samuels was the teacher at our district school. She was tall and slender and she wore her black hair in a little knot on the back of her head. She was as pretty as any woman in town, I guess, but it wasn't the kind of prettiness that seemed to go with bows and lace. She had a quiet beauty, and when she looked at you and smiled, you felt all sort of calm and peaceful. It was her eyes mostly that gave you that feeling. They were a deep blue, almost purple.

I never saw Miss Samuels get upset, not even when the big boys got in a fight in the schoolyard. She would walk right in among them, and she didn't even have to raise her voice to make them stop. She would just stand there quietly until they realized she was there. Then they would always stand still and look sort of shamefaced and unhappy. "I don't think either one of you is afraid of the other," she would say. "Now shake hands and be friends."

That was the way Miss Samuels was. She never scolded, and she never punished unless it just had to be done. Everybody in her classes tried to behave.

Grandpa said that Miss Samuels was one of the nicest things that had ever happened to our town. I guess everybody felt that way, especially the young men. Somehow, though, they never seemed to make much of an impression on Miss Samuels. She could have had beaus a-plenty, but she just didn't seem to bother.

Then one summer afternoon Miss Samuels met

Young Doc. It didn't begin very romantically. Miss Samuels took her Sunday School class on an outing near Village Creek. After they had eaten, some of the boys went fishing, and right off little Aubrey Williams man-.aged to stick a fishhook through the calf of his leg. The hook went right in the skin, with the barbed end coming out one side and the shank sticking out the other.

Nearly everybody tried to work that hook loose and pretty soon little Aubrey was squeeching and hollering every time anyone came near him. Finally he broke loose and climbed a persimmon tree. It took a long time for Miss Samuels to coax him down, but eventually they ended up sitting on the big leather sofa in Young Doc's office. Little Aubrey was bawling and Miss Samuels was white-faced.

Young Doc took one look at the hook, then walked to the door leading to the house and shouted to Black Bessie, his housekeeper. "Bessie, bring me the wire-cutters out of the tool box."

Little Aubrey started wailing louder at this and Miss Samuels got even paler.

"Surely," she said, "you're not—"

Young Doc didn't say anything. He just grunted. When he got the wire-cutters he made one quick snip and cut the eye off the hook. Then he pulled the smooth shank right out of the skin.

Little Aubrey and Miss Samuels both gasped and looked at each other in surprise. It seemed so easy.

Miss Samuels looked at Young Doc while he painted the wound with iodine. There was a twinkle in her eye. "Doctor, don't tell me they taught you things like that in medical school. You must have had a lot of experience with fishhooks when you were a boy."

Young Doc didn't say anything. He grunted again. The light died out of Miss Samuels' eyes. "No," she said, "I guess you didn't." She stood up and put her hand on Aubrey's shoulder. "Come, Aubrey."

When she got to the door, she turned. "Please send me the bill for your services, Doctor."

Young Doc was standing in the middle of his office, still holding the wire-cutters and the hook. "There'll be no charge," he said. He studied Miss Samuels a moment. "Tell me . . . what makes you think I didn't go fishing when I was a boy?"

Miss Samuels' voice was cool. "You aren't the type," she said. Then she walked out of the office, herding little Aubrey ahead of her.

I guess Miss Samuels was as surprised as anyone when she answered a knock on the door the next night and Young Doc was standing there, stern faced and stiff.

"Why, Doctor Harris . . ." Miss Samuels said.

Young Doc didn't waste any time. "Miss Samuels," he said, without a bit of expression on his face, "would you—that is—could you . . . er—go fishing with me to-morrow?"

Miss Samuels looked startled for a moment, then she smiled a little and her eyes twinkled. "Why, I'd be delighted," she said.

Young Doc relaxed a little. "That's fine," he said. "I'll call for you about ten o'clock." He turned and started across the veranda. When he reached the steps, he turned. "Bessie is packing us a lunch," he said. Then a small smile lit his face. "Thank you, Miss Samuels."

By the next day, everybody in Walesburg knew that Young Doc and Miss Samuels had gone fishing together. No one could quite figure that out, and more than one clacking tongue predicted that Miss Samuels soon would stop seeing Young Doc. They were wrong. Miss Samuels and Young Doc started keeping company regularly and they were seen almost everywhere, Miss Samuels smiling and at ease and Young Doc stiff and glum looking. You could always notice one thing wherever they were. Young Doc never took his eyes off Miss Samuels. Even if he was talking to someone else, you could see that he wasn't paying much attention. His eyes were on Miss Samuels.

A lot of folks said that Miss Samuels was teaching Young Doc to unbend a little. At first I thought so too, especially when she got him to come to church one Sunday. When they walked in I almost dropped through the pew with surprise. I looked up at Grandpa and I could see he felt the same way. Grandpa preached an extra fine sermon that Sunday. I don't guess Young Doc thought so. He sat there cold and unmoved.

On the way home I asked Grandpa about it. "Do you think Young Doc Harris will start comin' to church —do you, Grandpa?" Grandpa grinned.

"Son, what you saw today wasn't religion. What you saw was love." Then his face got sober. "It'll take a long time to make Young Doc Harris come to church. It's awfully hard to fight reason, son." And then he grinned again and took my hand. " 'Specially when it's bad reasonin'."

Grandpa was right. Young Doc never came to church except that one time. I guess even love couldn't make him change his mind about some things.

Nobody ever knew for sure just how Miss Samuels felt about Young Doc. I guess Grandpa and I were the first people in all of Walesburg to get a glimpse of it.

It happened on a day two weeks before school started. Grandpa was chairman of the school board and he had to go over to the school and inspect a new shingle roof that Clyde Ware had put on. It was a calm, peaceful day, and as I walked along with Grandpa I sighed because school would be starting so soon. Grandpa seemed to know how I felt, because once he looked at me and smiled.

"Son," he said, "I'm not goin' to take advantage of your good nature and tell you that these are the happiest days of your life. I guess you've heard that before, and I guess you doubt it. If I could make any impression on you, I'd just like to tell you that these are the days you will always remember as being the most fun. Life is like a mountain. Every time we get a little higher we can always stand for a moment and look back, and the goin' never seemed as rough as it does at the present."

"Don't people ever get to the top of the mountain, Grandpa?"

Grandpa chuckled. "Only if they are foolish," he said, "because then they have to start down again. The only thing worst than that is standin' still and complainin' that you can't go any farther. A slow, easy pull does it." Then he grinned and put his hand lightly on my shoulder. " 'Course, you have to watch your step."

"That sounds like some of the things you say in church, Grandpa."

Grandpa laughed again, and then he sighed and shook his head. "I guess you're right, son. Preachers are always preachin', I guess."

"It's a good thing they are," I said loyally.

"Yes, that's true," Grandpa said. "People need preachers more than they think," he chuckled, "but probably not nearly as much as some preachers think."

I must have looked surprised at this, because he patted me on the shoulder and went on: "What I mean is that a man is a man first and then a preacher. If he forgets he's a man and becomes just a psalm-singer, he's fightin' a losin' battle. You don't drive people to God, son, you lead them. And you don't lead them with a halter. Every man wants salvation. You just have to scratch pretty deep sometimes to find the urge."

"Young Doc Harris says he doesn't need religion," I said.

We walked for a while in silence before Grandpa spoke. "There's only one thing worse than a man who says he doesn't need religion," he said, "and that's a man who thinks he needs it too much. Religion isn't a crutch. It's an inspiration."

"Can people get along without religion, Grandpa?" I asked.

Grandpa looked down at me. "People can get along without eyes, son, but they can't see."

I was still turning that over in my mind when we reached the schoolyard. Our schoolhouse was all freshly painted, and with its new roof it looked so clean and neat that for a little while I forgot that I was sorry school was starting so soon. Grandpa and I walked around the building slowly, with Grandpa inspecting everything, and then we went inside. The inside of the school hadn't changed at all. It still smelled of chalk and blackboards and glue and ink. I stood in the doorway a minute and I could feel my feet getting itchy.

We had only been there a moment when Miss Samuels walked out of the cloakroom. Her hands were full of ink bottles and erasers. When she saw us she gave a little start and then she smiled. "Why, Parson Gray—and John—how nice!" She put the bottles and erasers on her desk and shook hands with us. "Whatever brings you to the school?" she asked.

"I had to look at the new roof, but I see Clem's done a good job, as usual," Grandpa said. Then he grinned slyly at me. "Anyway, John jest couldn't wait to get over to the school."

They both laughed and I managed to grin but I could feel my ears getting red.

Miss Samuels put her hand on my arm. "Don't you worry, John, it'll be summer again before you know it."

"I was tryin' to give him what comfort I could on the way over," Grandpa said, "but I think we got switched off on a discussion of religion."

"I can't think of a better topic on such a lovely day," Miss Samuels said. Then, all at once, we each seemed to think of the same thing. Miss Samuels was still smiling, but her eyes were grave. In the long silence, Grandpa cleared his throat a couple of times, and I shuffled my feet.

Finally Miss Samuels spoke. "I've been wanting to see you, Parson."

"Yes, Faith?" Grandpa said.

Her face was thoughtful. "It's . . . it's . . . well, it's just that some people have minds like . . . like carefully cultivated gardens. You know what I mean. Every row—every thought was planted carefully." She knitted her brows and made a little earnest gesture with her hands. "There's nothing bad about such minds. They are good, and kind and thoughtful. It's just that there's no more room for some things."

She looked a little sad. "Even love has to find its way in gradually . . . slowly. You do know what I mean, don't you?"

"Of course," said Grandpa.

Miss Samuels smiled. "Now I . . . I think I . . ." Suddenly, she became aware of my intent face and she was flustered. She half smiled and lowered her eyes.

I looked down at the floor, too, and then Grandpa coughed a little. "Hurmmph . . . hurmmph . . . son," he said, "would you go outside and finish inspectin' the roof? I'll be out directly."

I was glad to go. I walked out into the sunshine quickly. It was a problem I knew I couldn't handle.

For a while I chased a blue runner along the fence with a stick, and then I went around to the well behind the schoolhouse. It was a fine well, one of the deepest in the county. The water was always cold. It was still boarded up and I found a big rock and knocked the boards off the top. I went to the shed behind the school and fetched the big old, moss-covered wooden bucket that had been used for as long as I could remember. I didn't fasten the rope to the windlass but I let the bucket down into the cool depths of the well hand over hand. The water was as cool as ever, and after I had drunk all I wanted, I poured the rest over my head. Then I took the bucket back to the shed and again fastened back the cover.

As soon as I had finished I heard Grandpa calling me. I went around to the front door. Grandpa and Miss Samuels were standing there smiling, and I thought Miss Samuels looked awfully happy.

We told her good bye and started home. Grandpa walked quickly, not talking. Finally I couldn't hold it back any longer.

"Grandpa," I said, "did you and Miss Samuels talk about Young Doc?"

"Yes, son," Grandpa said.

"Is . . . is Miss Samuels going to make Young Doc change his mind?" I asked.

Grandpa shook his head slowly and shrugged. Then he smiled. "I don't rightly know, son—but I do know that love gets away with some things that preachers can't."

XII

PROFESSOR Jefferson Davis Jones came to Walesburg a week before school started. I was sitting on the front stoop eating syrup and bread when I first saw him. I almost choked. It wasn't Professor Jones as much as it was the contraption he was driving. I had never seen anything like it. It was a sort of surrey, except that it was bigger. It was almost the size of a covered wagon.

I sat open-mouthed, with the syrup running down my chin, while Professor Jones reined up at our gate. Then I could see that the wagon was painted red and gold, though a heavy layer of dust made it look brown. Across one side in big letters almost a foot high was printed: "Professor Jones, artist, conjurer and hypnotist—purveyor of Old Jones Lodestone Tonic—for Mothers, Babies, Old Folks & Animals."

While I sat there, too surprised to move, Professor Jones tied up his two tired bays and opened our gate. He was almost as odd as his wagon. He was a tall, lanky man and he wore a long-tailed frock coat, a white vest, a big cowboy hat and high-heeled cowboy boots. His nose was long and sharp. He had level black eyebrows and the darkest eyes I had ever seen. I was almost tempted to run. Then Professor Jones smiled and I changed my mind. It was a big broad smile. It made his face look almost boyish.

"Mornin', buckeroo," he said in a soft drawl, "yore pa to home?"

I gulped. "He's not . . . he's not my pa," I said, "he's my grandpa."

Professor Jones grinned again. "Could Ah chin with him?"

"Yes, sir," I stammered, "I'll . . . I'll fetch him."

I started to get up, but suddenly Professor Jones shoved his face so close to mine that I slumped back with surprise. "Hol' still," he said, and his eyes were wide, "somethin' stickin' outta yore ear."

My mouth was open. I sat there almost scared to breathe. He reached in my ear and pulled out a gold watch on a long chain, and dangled it in my face.

I felt hot all over. I jumped up and ran across the veranda. As I opened the front door, I looked back over my shoulder. Professor Jones was laughing so hard he had to hold his sides.

I found Grandpa in his study. I was so breathless I could hardly talk. "Grandpa," I said, "a man . . . a man pulled a watch out of my ear."

Grandpa was looking at some papers. He looked up absent-mindedly. "Yes," he said, "hmm—mm . . . hmm—mm." Then, suddenly, he realized what I had said. "What!" he said.

We walked out to the veranda and found Professor Jones sitting on the stoop, looking off into the distance. Grandpa looked at the Professor's wagon hitched at the gate and his eyebrows went up and he smiled. He cleared his throat. The Professor jumped up and turned around. He grinned when he saw me, peering at him from around Grandpa.

"Parson Gray?" he asked.

"Yes, suh," Grandpa said.

"Ah'm Jeff Davis Jones from the Panhandle o' Texas," the Professor said. "Ah'd be obliged to have a word with yo'."

They shook hands and Grandpa asked him into the house. I didn't let go of Grandpa's hand until we had settled in the study.

Professor Jones got right down to business. "Parson Gray, Ah've got a medicine show, as yo' probably noticed," he said, "an' Ah always make it a point to call on the parson in a town 'fore Ah give a performance."

Grandpa looked a little surprised, but he didn't say anything.

The Professor smiled. "Yo're probably a-wonderin' why. Wal, Parson, first off it's good bizness. If yo' get the leadin' citizen o' a town to come to yore show, then everybuddy else will come. Second, it's a promise Ah made to mah maw. Ah've got a Christian show an' Ah aim to keep it that way. Ah give a little music and

Ah give a little entertainment, an' Ah try to sell medicine. That's mah bizness, but Ah keep everythin' clean
and aboveboard."

It was easy to see the Professor was in dead earnest.

"How big is your show?" Grandpa asked.

"Wal, it ain't a circus, but it ain't a fly-by-night
outfit, either," Professor Jones said. "Thar's mahself
and ole Zeke and Young Frank, a couple of black boys,
who play the gittar and sing." He grinned again. "Ah'm
the feature attraction. Ah do magic tricks and try to
sell medicine. Parson, Ah'd shore be obliged if yo'
would come to mah show down by the depot tonight.
Ah'm prepared to give yore church ten per cent o' the
proceeds, if yo' do."

Grandpa sat there serious-faced, and my heart was
in my mouth. I wanted to see that show more than
anything.

Finally Grandpa shook his head. "I'm sorry, Mister
Jones," he said, "as much as I'd like to accept your kind
offer I can't. I can't lend mah services to your show,
even for a worthy cause. I do appreciate you comin'
to see me. It proves your good intent. If you want to
attend services at mah church next Sunday and put
something in the collection plate, that's your business."

Then Grandpa grinned. "And, of course, if I want
to come to your show tonight, that's mah business. I
don't promise I'll buy any medicine though."

Professor Jones smiled. "Thankee, Parson, Ah'll
do mahself proud. Hit's not always that a preacher
wants to come to a medicine show."

Grandpa chuckled at this. "I can't understan'

105

why," he said, "even angels like music." Then he looked at me where I sat beaming and almost popping with joy. "—Also small boys."

Grandpa and the Professor chatted for a few more minutes and then Grandpa asked: "Where were your folks from, Mister Jones?"

"Alabama," the Professor said, "down near Tuscaloosa. They moved to Texas after the wah."

"No doubt about which side your paw fought on, with that name of yours," Grandpa said.

"Reckon thar ain't," the Professor grinned, "but Ah think mostly hit was Uncle Perry's fault. Ah got mah itchin' feet from Uncle Perry. He was a ministrel man, and he could play *Dixie* on a gittar with both hands while he tooted *John Brown's Body* on the mouth organ."

We all laughed.

The Professor swelled up and all of a sudden it was like he was on a stage. "Yes, suh," he said, "mah Uncle Perry was the most musical man yo' ever seen. Durin' the wah, Uncle Perry was quite a bugle blower. In fact, he blowed the bugle in the fust Battle o' Bull Run. The only trouble—he blowed Retreat when he shoulda blowed Charge an' he sed we dern near lost that battle. Oncet we asked Uncle Perry 'bout the fust Battle o' Bull Run, an' he sed: 'Bull Run? Bull Run? Why, man, Bulls run, cows run, calves run—everybuddy run—all of 'em 'at didn't run is thar yit!"

Grandpa and I laughed until tears ran down our cheeks.

106

Then Professor Jones told us a joke about a railroad engine and a sawmill that got in an argument about which one could make the most noise. He could twist up his mouth and sound so much like both of them, snarling and tooting, that Grandpa and I almost fell off our chairs.

Finally he had to go, and we walked with him as far as the front stoop. I wasn't afraid at all now, and I stood right next to his side. He shook hands with Grandpa. Then he turned to me and looked surprised. "Buckeroo," he said, "what's that in yore nose?"

Before I could raise my hand or catch my breath, he tweaked my nose and a bright, shiny Indian-head penny fell on the floor. He picked it up and handed it to me. He shook his head and clucked. "Buckeroo, if Ah had yo', Ah'd start a joolry store."

Grandpa and I were still laughing when he got in his big old wagon and drove off.

"He's . . . he's nice . . . isn't he, Grandpa?" I asked.

"Yes, son," Grandpa said. He put his hand on my head. "He shares what he has."

"Yes, sir," I said, thinking about the bright new penny in my hand.

But I wasn't surprised when I heard Grandpa say: "Laughter."

I thought that day would never pass. At lunch I didn't eat much and Grandma looked at me closely. "I do declare," she said, "I never saw your eyes so bright." She put her hand on my forehead to see if I had fever, but Grandpa just chuckled. I laughed too, but the truth was that I wasn't feeling too well. My head felt light and sort of floaty and my stomach was heavy.

In the afternoon I sat on the porch and in just a little while the glare of the sun began to hurt my eyes. Finally I went out to the spring house and lay there in the coolness by the shelves loaded with Grandma's preserves and jellies. I felt better then, especially when I pressed my hot face against the cool ground. When I thought about Professor Jones and the show I was going to see that night, my head didn't hurt nearly as much. I must have fallen asleep because suddenly as plain as day I saw a big store. The shelves were so long that I could hardly see to the end of them. I looked up at the ceiling, but there wasn't any. The top of the store went right up to the sky and white clouds were floating by. I looked at my clothes and I was wearing a suit just like Professor Jones had, with cowboy boots and all.

Then a woman came in, all dressed up in jewels and with a long silk dress like in a mail-order catalog. "Is this a jewelry store?" she asked.

"Yes, ma'am," I said.

She put her face close to mine. "I want a gold watch," she said.

Her voice went echoing down the whole length of those long counters. "A gold watch . . . a gold watch . . . a gold watch."

"I don't have a watch," I said. "All I've got is a penny." I opened my hand to show it to her, but it was gone. Then the woman laughed and put her face closer to mine and I saw that she was really Professor Jones. "Here it is, buckeroo," he said. He reached in my ear and began to pull out watches. One right after another he pulled them out. "Watches . . . watches . . . watches," he laughed.

I laughed, too. I laughed until my sides hurt and suddenly I wasn't making laughing sounds at all. I was sounding like a sawmill, all screaming and snarling. "Look! Look!" I shouted, "I can go like a sawmill, too." I pursed up my mouth and let the sound roll out.

Then I was awake. It wasn't the sound of a sawmill at all. It was the spring house door squeaking as it opened. I opened my eyes and Grandpa was standing there. He seemed surprised to see me. "What's the matter, son?" he asked.

"Nothing," I said, and I grinned and shook my head. "I was asleep."

Grandpa looked at me. Then he reached down and put his hand on my head. It felt cool and nice.

"You feel feverish," Grandpa said.

"I got hot in the sun," I said.

Grandpa looked at me for a long moment, then he grinned and turned to the shelf and took down a jar of watermelon-rind preserves. "Come on," he said, "supper's nearly ready. Then we'll go to the show."

I couldn't eat much supper and Grandma fussed around over me like she always did when she thought I was getting sick. "Land sakes," she said, "I never saw such a boy! Eat your supper. That show will wait."

I ate everything on my plate just to please her, but it tasted dry and made me a little sick at my stomach. Even the watermelon preserves left a bad taste in my mouth. I was glad when supper was over.

It was just a little after dark when Grandpa and I left for the show. It was a cool, starry night with the smell of fall in the air and for a time I felt better. After we had walked a little way, Grandpa asked, "How do you feel, son?"

"All right," I said. I didn't want to think about feeling bad. I wanted to think about Professor Jones and the show. "Do you . . . do you think many people will come to the show tonight?" I asked.

Grandpa chuckled. "Son, I don't think there's any doubt about it," he said. " 'Bout as many people as come to church on Easter, I'll wager."

In just a few minutes we got within sight of the depot and I knew Grandpa was right. It looked like all Walesburg had turned out for that show. There wasn't much chance of them missing it. Professor Jones had hung lanterns on poles all over the field where he was holding his show and I had never seen anything so bright. Right in the middle of it all, the Professor had parked his big old surrey and then I saw why it was built the way it was. He had cleared out the seats and taken off the top and turned it into a stage. Big red banners were hanging from each end. They showed pictures of Indians in war paint with tomahawks.

The stage itself was all lit up with bright lamps with shiny silver reflectors. I was a little disappointed at what was on the stage, though, because all I could see was a little table covered with a green cloth. On top of it were a few cans and boxes. There were two poles at each end of the stage and hanging from them were charts showing nerves and muscles in the human body.

I had seen the same sort of pictures in Dr. Gilroy's Home Remedy book which Grandpa kept in his study.

Grandpa and I went through the crowd, with him stopping ever so often to shake hands with someone. A lot of people smiled and spoke to me, too, and I tried to grin back, but I had a hard time. There was a buzzing in my head now and the lights hurt my eyes. My supper wasn't sitting well at all, and I had to swallow hard a couple of times to keep from getting sick at my stomach.

Finally Grandpa and I had moved up right close to the stage. As we stood there the lights started dancing before my eyes. I was hoping that we wouldn't have long to wait.

We didn't. Suddenly there was a lot of clapping and then the crowd began to laugh. Professor Jones' two colored helpers had climbed up on the stage and everybody was laughing because they were dressed in Indian war clothes. They had on big feathered war bonnets and fringed buckskin suits. They even had war paint on and it looked awfully bright against their black faces. They were grinning as they took their places at each end of the platform. Then I saw that they each carried guitars. They stood there for a minute to let the crowd get a good look at them and then one of them stomped his foot three times and they started strumming away on the guitars. It wasn't a tune. It was a long, loud rolling sound and it got higher and higher. Everybody started clapping and whistling. I wanted to join in, but my head hurt too much.

When the strumming got so loud it seemed the

111

guitars would fall apart, it suddenly stopped. Professor Jones stepped onto the stage. I had never seen anybody like him outside of books. He looked like Buffalo Bill and Daniel Boone all at the same time. He had on a white buckskin suit and it was shining and glistening with hundreds of little red and blue beads. The fringe on his jacket shimmered like silver. Dangling from his hips were two fancy six-guns with ivory handles and bright red tassels at the end. Everybody sort of gasped when they saw him. Then they began to clap and whistle so loud that big waves of sound beat against my head. Professor Jones made a couple of whirls around the small stage and the clapping got louder. After he had given everybody a good look, he held up both hands and the noise gradually died down.

The Professor grinned and then he looked down at his clothes sort of sadly. "Hit's a shame what a full-grown man'll do to earn a livin', hain't it?" he shouted. Everybody roared. That's all I heard. He talked on for a long time, but his voice sounded far away. I guess he was funny because the crowd kept laughing, but I was so sick that I thought I would fall on the ground. Water was rushing to my mouth and I had to keep swallowing so fast that I thought I would choke.

After a few minutes it seemed like all that noise and those lights were falling on me. I was going down . . . down . . . down.

"Grandpa . . . Grandpa," I gulped, and my voice sounded high and funny.

I felt Grandpa's arm tight around my shoulders, and then the sickness came—again and again.

I thought I would lose my breath, but every time I gasped I got sick again. Everything was just black and far away and I wanted to lie down. Far away I could hear people talking. I could even hear the Professor going on and on.

Then I heard somebody say something about a buggy, and then before I knew it I could feel Grandpa carrying me. I knew it was Grandpa because I could feel his arms and the fabric of his coat. I tried to hold close to him. I must have gone to sleep.

When I woke up Grandma was undressing me and making little clucking sounds. "It was the excitement. I knew it was the excitement."

Grandpa's voice sounded like it was in the next room, it was that far away. "No, Harriet," he said. "He's sick. Doc Harris will be here directly."

I wanted to say that I didn't want Doc Harris, but I was too tired. The bed felt warm and deep. I closed my eyes. A cloud came by and I floated away.

XIII

AT first there was a band around my head. I felt it pressing tighter and tighter. I thought my head would split. I reached to pull the band away, but I couldn't find it. I buried my face in my hands for a long time. When finally I took them away, I couldn't see anything. Gradually, it began to get lighter. The light seemed to

come down from above. It whirled around . . . around
. . . around, swirling and gurgling like water going down
a drain. Then I saw I was in a cave. It was deep and
dank. My heart started pounding from fright. I opened
my mouth and tried to holler but no sound came. I
strained and strained until I thought my throat would
swell up and burst. Still no sound came.

I began to get hot. At first it was a fiery blast on
my face and hands. After that the heat seemed to get
inside my body. It spread into my stomach and my head
and my toes. I could hardly breathe. I threw myself
on the ground and lay there moaning. My mouth was
dry. Then it began to get sticky. I thought I would
choke.

My tongue was swollen and I was gasping for
breath when I heard the sound of running water. The
sound came closer and closer. The very gurgle seemed
to explode in my head.

Suddenly, I realized I wasn't in a cave at all. I was
lying in a meadow. The sun was beating down on me.
I had never felt the sun so hot. It made my head hurt.
It dazzled my eyes. I squinted and clenched my jaws
tight. Then I saw the water. It was running in a broad
stream right near my face. The water was rippling
along, blue and cold. I buried my face in the stream and
began to drink with long, breath-taking gulps. I drank
for a long time before I realized I couldn't taste the
water. It was going down my throat and I felt heavy
inside, but I couldn't taste it. My thirst was worse than
ever.

"Water! Water!" I moaned. My voice went

higher—"Water! *Water! Water!*" Suddenly I was soaring with my voice. I could see ice-capped mountains below and the tops of cool cedars and pines. "I've got to get down!" I thought. "I've got to get down!"

Then I wasn't in the air at all. I was lying in our barn, covered with cottonseed hulls. They were in my nose and mouth. They were crawling and wiggling. I opened my mouth and tried to scream, but the cottonseeds crawled in. They were coming in a long stream. They were choking me. I went down . . . down . . . down. Water. Ice. Water! Cedars. Pines. Sun. Hot. Hot. Water! Water! Water!

I never knew how long that lasted, but pretty soon I realized quiet hands were taking care of me. They were cool and gentle. I knew it must be Grandma. I felt better and after a while I opened my eyes. I was surprised to find myself back in my room. But the strangest thing was that Young Doc Harris was the first person I saw. I knew it was his hands I felt. He had taken off his coat and rolled back the sleeves of his white shirt. He was sponging off my body with a damp cloth. I looked at his stern face in the lamplight for a long time. Before I drifted off again I remember how strange it was that a man's face could be so hard—and his hands so gentle.

There were other times I remember, too. Once I opened my eyes and saw Grandma sitting by the bed. It must have been late because she was dozing in her chair. The light was shining in her white hair. I thought she looked like an angel in the picture books with a big halo. I wanted to wake her up and tell her so, but I couldn't. Something started pulling me down again, and I was too tired to fight back.

It must have been later when I awakened and saw Grandpa. I opened my eyes and the room was dark. Grandpa was standing at the foot of my bed. He had his hands on the footboard and his eyes were lifted upward. He looked just like he did when he led the prayers in church. I just had to try to talk to him.

After a long time, somehow I managed to swallow hard and open my mouth. "I'm . . . I'm . . . all . . . all right," I said.

Grandpa looked down quickly. I tried to grin. He looked at me a long time and then he smiled. He had to hold his lips tight when he did it. Then he winked. But there was something about his eyes that worried me. I wanted to ask Grandpa what had happened. But I was too tired. I dozed off again.

Sometime after that, things began to take shape again. I remember the fragments of a dozen scenes and conversations but everything seemed blurry and far away. It was like holding Grandpa's old spyglass to your eye. At first things were fuzzy, but after a while you worked it right, and everything got clear and close. That was the way it was with me. One day I woke up and the sun was streaming into my room. I lay there for a long time, listening to the sounds of the day. Then suddenly I remembered I hadn't eaten in a long time. I felt that I was starving. "Grandma! Grandma!" I yelled.

Grandma was in the next room. I heard the patter

of her feet as she came running. "Land sakes," she was saying. "Land sakes."

When she came into the room she was breathless and excited. "I'm hungry," I said. Grandma just stood there wide-eyed, looking at me. "Could . . . could I have a biscuit and some syrup?" I asked.

She started crying at that, but all she could say was, "Land sakes—land sakes."

Grandma fixed me some broth and both she and Grandpa came in while I ate it. They were both grinning. I ate the broth and asked for some more. They shook their heads.

"I was sick yesterday, wasn't I?" I asked.

Grandpa and Grandma looked at each other. Then Grandpa spoke, "You've been sick a week, son."

I couldn't believe that. "A whole week!" I said, looking to see if they were joshing.

They nodded.

"Was . . . was it something I ate?"

Grandpa shook his head. "No, son, you had slow fever. We're thankful to the Lord that you didn't have it bad. You threw it off awfully quick."

I lay there and thought about that. "Slow fever . . . slow fever—what causes it, Grandpa?"

"The real name is typhoid," Grandpa said. "You probably drank some creek water when you went fishin' with Uncle Famous."

"No, sir, I never did," I said.

Grandpa and Grandma just smiled, like I could have been mistaken. But I knew I wasn't.

117

It was that night before I thought about school. Grandma was feeding me some more broth and Grandpa was sitting in a rocker at the foot of the bed. "What's today?" I asked between sips.

"Saturday," Grandma said.

"I . . . I go to school Monday."

Grandma smiled and wiped some broth off my chin. She shook her head. "I'm afraid you'll be a little late this year," she said.

That surprised me. "How late?" I asked.

"Two . . . maybe three weeks," Grandma said.

I thought that over a little while. "That's too bad," I said.

Grandpa coughed at that and Grandma squeezed her lips tight and started fussing around like she always did when she didn't want to laugh at something I did. "Land sakes, eat your broth. I never saw such a boy!" Then she sort of giggled and Grandpa coughed some more.

I grinned too, but the funny thing was—I really was sorry.

Even if I hadn't known the next day was Sunday, I could have told from the sound of things. Sunday was the big day of the week in our house. Grandpa was singing *Lead, Kindly Light* while he stirred around, dressing to go to church. Grandma was bustling around in the kitchen fixing breakfast, and at the same time keeping an ear tuned toward upstairs. That was because ever so often Grandpa would quit singing and we'd hear him opening and shutting drawers and mumbling while he looked for his socks or gold collar button.

Finally he would give up and call to Grandma for help. Grandma would sigh then and go on and find what Grandpa wanted.

"Land sakes, if it had been a rattlesnake, it would have bitten you," she would say.

Grandpa would chuckle at that. "Now, Harriet," he'd say, "you know you hide things." Then before Grandma could say anything else, he'd start booming *Lead, Kindly Light* again.

Grandma always said that she could have gotten Grandpa's whole congregation ready for church quicker than she could him. That would make Grandpa grin. He would smooth down his pulpit coat and throw back his shoulders and wink at me. "Now, now, Harriet," he would say, "you've got to admit the result is worth the bother."

That usually made Grandma sniff a little, but her eyes would shine and I knew she really thought it was the truth, even if Grandpa was joshing.

Grandpa looked especially nice when he came into my room before leaving for church. His white hair was brushed back and his face was shining like it always did right after he got through shaving.

"Reckon you'll both be playin' hookey from church today," he said.

Grandma cut her eyes at him. "I just hope you can get along without us, Mister Gray."

" 'Course," Grandpa said. "I'll get a chance to tell some of mah Irish stories."

Grandma caught her breath. "Don't you dare, Mister Gray," she said.

Grandpa laughed. His Irish stories had always been a joke ever since he was a young preacher and the presiding elder had visited his church. Grandpa wanted to make a good impression and he tried to lighten up his sermon with a few stories. He was trying to show that people should respect the rights of their neighbors and he told about an old maid who had gone to a steamship office to plan a vacation. The clerk was a red-headed Irishman named O'Reilly.

The first place O'Reilly suggested was South America. The old maid sniffed. "I don't think I want to go to South America," she said. "I understand there are a lot of Indians and half-breeds down there. No, I don't want to go to South America. And I may as well tell you that there's one other place I don't want to go. I don't want to go to Ireland. They tell me that it's cold and wet and full of Catholics."

That was too much for O'Reilly. "Faith an' begorra, Miss," he said, "suppose you go to Hell. It's hot and dry and full of Protestants."

Grandpa thought it was a good story and so did his congregation. But the presiding elder almost fell out of his chair from shock.

Afterward at dinner he called Grandpa down. "Young man," he said, between bites of Grandma's fried chicken, "I think you should realize that a church is no place for laughter."

Grandma was a young bride and she was scared half to death, but Grandpa didn't seem to be worried one bit.

"If people can't laugh in church," he said, "laughter must be wrong—an' I don't think it is."

The presiding elder got stiff as a ramrod. "It's not the sound of laughter, it's the cause of laughter to which I am objectin'," he said.

Grandpa kept on eating calmly. "I didn't see anything wrong with mah story."

That made the presiding elder so mad, he started waving a half-gnawed drumstick. "You actually said *Hell* in that story!" he said.

Grandpa raised his eyebrows. "The only place I know where a man can say Hell in mixed company, elder—is when he's standin' in a pulpit."

The presiding elder was mad as a hornet and he left right after dinner. Grandma worried a lot about what might happen, but Grandpa said the only thing that worried him was that the elder might get indigestion from eating too fast.

"How you do talk," Grandma said. "He can get you transferred to another church next conference."

Grandpa raised his eyebrows. "Get me transferred? Why, that's mah church. The people gave it to me an' nobody can take it away unless they do."

"Oh, yes, they can," Grandma said. "The Conference can send you packin' off to Timbuctoo if it wants to. What would you do if you were ordered to another church?"

Grandpa grinned. "Reckon we'd jest have to secede," he said. "I reckon if the Southern Methodist can secede from the Northern Methodist—then it stan's to reason that one little church can secede from the Southern Methodist." Then Grandpa laughed, but Grandma was never sure whether it was a joke or not.

Anyway, nothing ever happened, except that Grandma always got nervous when Grandpa would smile in the middle of a sermon and say, "That reminds me of an Irish story . . ."

Just before Grandpa left for church, Aunt Pim came by. I could hear her and Grandma chattering away as they came up the stairs. Grandpa cocked his head and listened and then he smiled at me. "Looks like I've lost another sheep from mah flock this Sunday."

He was right. Aunt Pim came in and made a fuss over me as she always did, and then she turned to Grandpa. "J. D. Gray," she said, "you'll have to get along without me today. John and I have been havin' a visit every Sunday for a long time, an' I reckon this Sunday isn't goin' to be any different."

Grandpa grinned. "We'll miss your sweet voice," he said.

Aunt Pim snorted, but she was pleased. "Sometimes you soun' like a ribbon drummer," she said.

After Grandpa had left for church, Aunt Pim and Grandma brought their rockers in my room and sat there talking. I lay still, half-listening and half-dozing. I felt good, hearing the hum of their voices and smelling Grandma's dinner cooking in the kitchen.

"Young Doc Harris stayed heah for three hours taking care of John one night," Grandma said.

Aunt Pim made a clucking sound. "I do declare. He is a good man, I believe, though I must say he's not nearly as friendly as his father."

"No," said Grandma, "but I do believe Faith Samuels is getting him to unbend a little."

"Maybe they'll get married," Aunt Pim said.

There was doubt in Grandma's voice. "I don't know. It could happen, but I sort of think Faith is lookin' for a straight stick."

They talked on for a little while, but I wasn't listening. Something Grandma had said had snagged my mind. Finally I got so curious I couldn't hold it back any longer. "What's a straight stick, Grandma?" I asked.

Grandma stopped right in the middle of what she was saying. Both she and Aunt Pim laughed. "Such a boy," Grandma said. "He hears everything."

"I guess it does soun' funny at that," Aunt Pim said.

"I guess it does," said Grandma. Then, while Aunt Pim listened and nodded every once in a while, Grandma told me what she meant. When she and Aunt Pim were young girls Grandma wasn't satisfied with any of the young men who came calling. She made jokes about them and laughed at the way they acted.

Finally Grandma's mother decided that she needed a talk. "One time, Harriet," she said, "I knew a man who went walking in the woods, looking for a stout limb to make into a walking stick. He hadn't gone far before he saw what looked like a proper oak limb. He started to cut it when he noticed that it had the slightest curve. 'I'll just look a little longer,' the man decided. Next he came to an ash tree and spied a limb that seemed just right. The man raised his axe before he noticed that limb was curved a tiny bit, too. It wasn't bent quite as much as the first one, but still the man decided to look a little longer. Next was a hickory tree. The limb the man saw there had just a slight curve, but he didn't take it. One after another, this man went through the woods inspecting limbs and discarding them because they had the slightest imperfection. The first thing he knew it was dark. He had spent a whole day in the forest and he didn't have anything to show for his time."

Grandma smiled. "Mama said that was the way I was about men. 'Harriet,' she said, 'every man has some little defect. If you're lookin' for a perfect man—you'll never find him.'"

After Grandma had told me the story, she and Aunt Pim sat there smiling at each other with happy memories shining in their eyes. Then Grandma shook her head. "I may not have gotten a perfectly straight stick, but I'm sure I got the nearest thing to it."

Aunt Pim had a far-away look in her eyes as she nodded slowly.

I felt awfully sad looking at her. "Aunt Pim . . . well, Aunt Pim had a straight stick, too," I said, thinking of Captain Hall.

Aunt Pim got red in the face at that and bit at her lips and looked down at the floor. I could see Grandma was flustered too. She tried not to show it, but she stood up quickly. "I do declare," she said, "I believe I hear Mister Gray comin' home from church—an' so soon." She walked out of the room.

I looked at Aunt Pim and tears were standing in her eyes. She smiled at me and I smiled back. But I was wondering. For the first time I realized that Grandma never would talk about Captain Hall or Aunt Pim's tree.

124

XIV

GRANDPA always said that a man didn't appreciate a corn until he lost his feet. On the morning that school opened I knew what he meant. As I lay in bed listening to Old Gabriel crow at the sun and brag in front of all the hens, I felt sad and sort of lost. It gave me a lonesome feeling to know that all over Walesburg other children were up and getting ready for school whilst I had to stay there in bed.

For as long as I could remember I had been going to school on opening day. Even when I was too little to go to classes, Grandpa used to take me with him when he went down to open the term with a prayer. Everybody in Walesburg, even full-grown men like Perry Lokey and Amos Ware, used to say that they remembered Grandpa opening school more than they did some of the things they studied. It was easy to see why. After the invocation, Grandpa used to make a little talk. It would end up with everybody laughing and giggling. Even the scared little beginners always felt better.

Grandpa always took a big interest in our school. He was especially careful to pick good teachers. Mostly it was because of the kind of teachers he had as a boy. One of them used to stand by the door on opening day with a big cane. As the pupils came through the narrow door, the teacher would whack each one of them across the back with the cane. When they looked up in surprise and fright, the teacher would wave the cane and say, "That's jest to show you who's a-runnin' this school."

This same teacher acted as the preacher on Sunday. Grandpa said that many's the time he heard him preach a two-hour sermon on love and then go out and kick a dog half to death because it would come up and sniff at his boots.

Grandpa went to that school until he was sixteen. Then his little sister started to school and they entered the doorway on opening day together. The schoolteacher swung down with his cane—whack! right across Grandpa's little sister's shoulders.

Grandpa used to chuckle when he told that part of the story. "I reckon I started on my higher education then," he said.

"What . . . what happened, Grandpa?" I asked.

"Oh," said Grandpa, lightly, "we got a new schoolteacher."

"What . . . what happened to the old one?" I asked, wide-eyed.

"He was almost worn out," Grandpa said. Then he turned and looked at me and there was a twinkle in his eye. "His walkin' cane was all the way worn out!"

When Grandpa told me stories like that it would scandalize Grandma. "Mister Gray," she would say, "I don't think you should tell that child such things."

"No," said Grandpa, "I reckon I shouldn't." Then he chuckled. "I reckon it's a bad example. He might think he's got to wait until he's sixteen to take care of bullies."

"Land sakes," sighed Grandma, but she giggled.

I was thinking about all this when Grandpa came into my room bringing my breakfast on Grandma's big old silver platter. Right away he must have seen how I felt because he grinned at me and shook his head. "Don't worry, son, you'll be back in school 'fore you know it."

I started eating my grits and trying to act like I didn't care. "I'm not worrying," I said.

Grandpa chuckled at this. "No," he said, "I guess you aren't." He paused by the door a minute. "In fact, I'm probably one of the few people in Walesburg who's headed for the school house this morning, who feels good about it."

I laughed at that, and then Grandpa said, "Well, anyway keep those wild-cat traps clean," and he was gone.

Somehow I felt better after Grandpa said that. It was a joke between us ever since I had started to school in the first grade. I could never forget that morning. I was half scared to death and my stomach was jumping like I had swallowed a frog. Grandma had bought me a blue serge suit. I was pleased as punch with the way I looked when I came to the breakfast table. Grandpa was eating away like nothing unusual was happening, and I tried to act unconcerned too. But it was Grandma that worried me. Her face was red and she kept dabbing at her eyes with her apron. I tried to swallow my breakfast and act as if I had been going to school every day of my life.

Finally breakfast was over and Grandpa shoved back his chair. I did too, and we looked at each other for a long time. Then Grandpa cleared his throat and looked at his big old watch. "We'd best be goin'," he said.

When he said that, Grandma sniffed out loud and I knew what was wrong. Grandma was crying. That scared me. I swallowed hard. "What's wrong, Grandma?"

Grandma just screwed up her face and then buried it in her apron. It was Grandpa who spoke. "Your Grandma is just passin' another milestone, son." Then he went over and put his arm around her shoulders. "Now, now, Harriet," he said, "John'll feel bad."

I was open-mouthed with wonder. "Don't . . . don't you want me to go to school, Grandma?" If she had made the slightest sign I was ready to call the whole thing off.

Grandma blew her nose hard and looked at me for a long time. "Land sakes!" she said. " 'Course I want you to go to school. Now pull up your stockin's and put some water on that cowlick. Such a boy!"

There was something different about going to school. I knew it the minute Grandpa and I left the house. He didn't hold my hand like he usually did. I walked along by his side, trying to take big strides like he did. I sort of felt grownup with my new suit and when we passed other children I was glad Grandpa wasn't holding my hand.

When we got to the school house I already knew what bench to take. I had been there so many times. Lots of the beginners were there with their mamas and they were acting timid and shy like they always did. I guess I sort of swaggered. I kept looking at the other beginners and smiling like the second-graders on the bench behind me.

I guess that was a mistake. Before long Bart Benefield, who was in the second grade, leaned over and hissed in my ear. "You're a sissy in a store-bought suit." I tried to act like I didn't hear him but I could feel my ears getting red. I heard Bart whispering to some other boys and they started giggling. That made me red in the face. For a minute I almost wanted to get up and go up to Grandpa on the platform.

Then somebody behind me kicked me with the toe of his shoe and I almost fell off the bench. At first I thought Grandpa had seen that. For the barest second he looked my way, but then he turned and started talking to Miss Samuels.

That was the worst time of my life. All through Grandpa's prayer and speech those boys kept nudging me with their toes and ever so often Bart Benefield would lean close and whisper: "You're a sissy. Sissy!"

I was sweating and beet-red by the time the ceremony was over. I felt so bad that I wanted to cry. I dreaded the time when Grandpa would leave me there alone.

Finally it was all over, though, and everybody clapped and Miss Samuels and Grandpa shook hands. Grandpa came down off the platform. For a minute I thought he was going to pass me by. Then he turned like it was an afterthought and came up to where I was sitting. The nudging and whispering stopped.

Grandpa looked straight at me, but his voice was loud enough to be heard for three rows. "Well, John," he said, "I'll go on home now—but you hurry on as soon as school is out. We'll have to clean those traps if we're goin' wild-cat huntin' tonight." All those kids behind me gasped and I could hear Bart Benefield whispering in awe, "Wile cat! Garfield! Wile cat!"

Grandpa stuck out his hand to me like I was a full-grown man. I took it and shook it—but I could have kissed him.

Sometimes Grandpa said that if he hadn't decided to be a preacher, he would have liked to have been a teacher. He claimed there really wasn't much difference. He explained it to me while we were sitting on the veranda one night. "A teacher, son," he said, "can prove to you that two and two are four. We preachers can prove that evil never equals anything, 'cept evil, an' good never equals anything but good." Then Grandpa chuckled. "The big fault is that we preachers can't prove it with apples. It's a funny thing—everybody can see the rules of arithmetic, but some people jest can't total up the benefits of right livin'."

Grandpa sighed. "Sometimes I think it's because they lose sight of the broad aims of religion. You don't put on religion with your Sunday clothes, an' you don't forget it when you lay down your Bible or hymn book. You carry it inside of you. It's a way of life—not an exact science that you have to keep analyzin'. Some people can't see that. They make too much of the things they can't see, an' not enough of the things they can see.

"When I was a young man I heard a brilliant mathematician get up and say flatly that he didn't think God had anything to do with makin' the Universe. In fact, he didn't think God had anything to do with anything—because he didn't believe in God. He said that the Allegheny Mountains once were about thirty thousand feet high. They have been cut down by ice and snow and rain and carried away in rivers until they are now only about six thousand feet high. He smirked an' asked me if the Creator wanted them to be six thousand feet high —why didn't He make them that way in the first place?"

Grandpa shook his head. "I didn't know an' I told him so. Then I asked him if he could trisect an angle. He said certainly not, nobody could. 'Well,' I said, 'you can divide a hundred in three parts—you can even cut an apple into three parts. Why can't you trisect an angle?' He said it was a mathematical impossibility. Then I asked, 'Well, jest because there is one unsolved mystery in mathematics, do you say that two an' two doesn't make four?' He said certainly not. 'Why in

Heaven's name then,' I asked, 'are you disputin' the existence of God simply because you can't understan' why the snow and rains and ice whittled down the Allegheny Mountains?' He thought mah argument was foolish. 'Course that made us even. I felt the same way 'bout his."

Grandpa sat quietly for a long time before he spoke again. "You know, son, there are a lot of people who deny God simply because they say they can't find out where Cain got his wife, or because they say the whale couldn't have swallowed Jonah. 'Course that's not their real reason, an' they know it. I guess it's a way of thinkin'. As far as I'm concerned, I can look at a rose covered with dew or watch a young mother tendin' her baby an' know there's a God. Things like that would be proof enough, even if I didn't know more. People who want to believe in God always can find Him. An' they don't have to wait until they die to know that He's real."

Grandpa went on. "That's why preachers are really teachers. They aren't blazin' new trails, or doin' research. They're jest teachin' some old truths, an' it always adds up to the same—jest like the multiplication table. The most advanced, enlightened modern man an' the old Christian starin' a hungry lion in the face aren't different at all, in that respect."

"Then . . . why is it that people go to different churches, Grandpa?"

Grandpa smiled. "Because people are people, son. They're different—an' for the same reason that every town has more than one road leadin' into it—every house has more than one door. People may travel different roads, but if they travel them right—they end up in the same place. An' they carry the same feelin' in their hearts. Lots of folks think that people come to church to be reassured. They don't. When they begin to doubt, they stay away. People come to church to pay their respects in the way they think is best. They come to church to find new ways of realizin' old truths.

"If I had my way, I would have liked to have been a minister to children. When you give a man an idea—it's jest, well—it's jest an idea. It usually stays whole and intact. But when you give a child an idea, it's like plantin' a seed in the spring. It grows and grows. It's watered by curiosity and it's warmed by reflection. Young minds are rich soil." Grandpa chuckled. "People are always talkin' about the simplicity of a child's faith. Sometimes they get that simplicity confused with gullibility. Why, bless it all, son—a young mind accepts nothin'. Who is it who's always askin' what makes the grass green, or what holds the stars up, or why is the moon shiny? It's always a child. Full-grown people never ask those things, though most of them don't know the answers. Yes, sir, you let me plant the right ideas in the minds of children, an' I'll reap a rich harvest."

I lay in bed, thinking about that talk with Grandpa for a long time. Then I must have dozed off because the next thing I knew I heard the front door open and Grandpa's footsteps in the hall. I knew something was wrong by the sound. I heard Grandma's voice, "Wasn't that Young Doc Harris in front of the house . . . why, Mister Gray, what on earth is your face so red about?"

Grandpa's voice seemed to be half tired and half mad. "Yes, that was Young Doctor Harris," he said. "He was comin' in, but he decided not to when I told him John was feelin' better and eatin'."

Mister Gray," Grandma said, "I hope y'all didn't have words."

"No," Grandpa said, and his voice sounded resigned, "we didn't have words. But do you know he had the nerve to tell me that I endangered those children by goin' down to the schoolhouse today! He seemed downright shocked that I went."

"What on earth . . . ?" said Grandma, surprised.

"He said that I was liable to spread John's slow fever. He even got that sassy look when I told him that I held services at the church yesterday. What does he expect?"

"Why, I never!" said Grandma.

"I never did, either," said Grandpa. He sighed so loud I heard it upstairs. "All I hope, Harriet, is that I get to the gates of Heaven before Young Doc Harris. If I don't—I do believe that he won't let me in!"

XV

ILLY-ELLY CARROLL was the fastest reader in our school. The trouble was that nobody ever knew what he was saying. When the other children would get up to read and stumble over a hard word, Miss Samuels could correct them from her desk. When Illy-Elly came to a word he didn't know, he had to take his book up to Miss Samuels and point it out. That was because Illy-Elly was tongue-tied and nobody ever quite knew where he was until he turned a page. Even then they couldn't follow him except for maybe a word or two.

Sometimes the other children sniggered at Illy-Elly, but that didn't seem to bother him at all. He was just my age, but he was a lot smaller. He was fat and somehow his shirttail always managed to sneak out of his overalls. He always had a grin on his freckled face and everybody liked him. Even when the older boys teased him or asked him to read for them, they did it kindly.

Illy-Elly's real name was Sam but nobody except Miss Samuels called him that because of something that happened the first week he started to school. During recess Illy-Elly got to wrestling around with Hugh Renfroy and Willie Baxter. They weren't scuffling rough, just sort of playing around until suddenly Illy-Elly fell sprawling, face down, right on Willie. That must have hurt Willie, but the funny thing was that Illy-Elly gave out with a squeech. He hollered so loud that even Miss Samuels heard it. She came running.

Illy-Elly was sitting on the ground, holding his stomach and crying as loud as he could. Willie and Hugh were standing off to one side, looking scared and ashamed.

"What's wrong, Sam?" Miss Samuels asked.

Illy-Elly didn't stop squalling, but he pointed a finger at Hugh and Willie.

Miss Samuels turned in surprise. "Why, boys," she said, "why did you hurt Sam?"

Illy-Elly was still crying, but he managed to stop long enough to explain to Miss Samuels. "Hue—he all rith," he sobbed, "but 'Illy—'Illy bite me on the 'elly!" Then he started wailing again while he pulled up his shirt and showed Miss Samuels the teeth marks.

That was the way Illy-Elly got his nickname. For a long time the big boys would come up to him grinning and say, "Show us where 'Illy bit you on the 'elly." Pretty soon they just got to calling him Illy-Elly.

I guess I hadn't thought of Illy-Elly all summer until the morning Grandpa came from town and walked into the kitchen. I was sitting at the table, looking at the pictures in Grandpa's copy of *Pilgrim's Progress*. Grandma was baking gingerbread. It was three weeks since I had been taken sick. I was planning on going back to school the next Monday.

Grandpa's face was grave when he came in, and right away I knew something was wrong. He spoke to me. "Son, little Sam Carroll died this mornin'."

At first I was too shocked to say anything. It didn't seem possible. I heard Grandma say, "Oh, merciful Heaven!"

I looked at Grandpa closely to see if it were some sort of a strange joke.

"Illy-Elly Carroll?" I said.

Grandpa nodded. "Yes, son."

"But . . . how—why? . . ." I began.

Grandpa's voice was low. "It was slow fever. He'd just been sick a week. It carried him right out."

Grandma started untying her apron. "I'd better go," she said.

"No, Harriet," Grandpa said. "I went by the house on my way home."

"Oh, that poor Miz Carroll," Grandma said.

I just couldn't seem to say anything. I was that stunned. It was the first time that anybody I had known had died, except for grown people. I thought about fat little Illy-Elly. It just didn't seem possible.

Grandpa sat down at the table and looked off into space like he was thinking. "Harriet," he said, "I learned this mornin' that six other children at the school are down with slow fever."

"Mercy!" said Grandma in surprise. "What does Young Doc—" Then Grandma stopped suddenly. She looked at me and I looked at her. I knew we were both thinking the same thing. I turned to Grandpa. He seemed to be deep in thought. He drummed his fingers on the table a second.

"I haven't heard from Doctor Harris," he said, "but I feel sure—I know—I will."

They buried Illy-Elly Carroll the next day. Grandpa conducted the funeral services and Grandma attended. But they wouldn't allow me to go.

Grandpa called me into his study and explained. "We just don't want to take any chances until you're completely well," he said. Then he put his hand on my shoulder. "I'm sorry you can't go to the church to pay respects to Sam but people will understan'—and anyway you can do it just as well heah."

"How?" I asked.

"By your memories of him," Grandpa said.

I thought that over for a long time after Grandpa and Grandma had left for the church. I didn't like to be alone in the house so I wandered out to the back porch and sat on the stoop. Pretty soon I heard the organ at Grandpa's church start playing softly. I knew the services for Illy-Elly had begun. Then I thought about one day when we played a game in school. Everybody in my class had to get up behind Miss Samuels' desk and act out in pantomime what they wanted to be when they grew up.

When it was my turn I got up and used the desk as a pulpit. Right off everybody guessed I wanted to be a preacher. I suppose they would have known anyway, because of Grandpa. Kim Aldridge got up and held his arms as if he were holding a plow. Right away we all shouted: "Farmer." Bert Justin went up and made motions on the desk until somebody realized he was using it as an operating table. He admitted he wanted to be a doctor.

Illy-Elly was next. He had a big grin on his freckled face when he went to the front of the room. He held one arm straight in front of him, and he kept pulling the other one back and forth. Nobody could guess what he wanted to be. Even the upper classes got interested after a while. Miss Samuels let them try to guess, though they were supposed to be studying. Finally Susie Gailbraith thought she had the answer. She was almost grown and about to graduate. "He wants to be a musician," she said. "He's playing a harp."

Illy-Elly shook his head. His fat little body was wiggling with joy and excitement. He was happy because he had everybody guessing.

After a long time everybody gave up. Not even Miss Samuels could guess what Illy-Elly wanted to be. "You win, Sam," she said. "Tell us what you want to be."

Illy-Elly's face got serious. "Thith ith a bow an' arrer," he said. "I wanth to be an Indian!"

When I thought about that day I lay back on the porch and giggled. Suddenly I remembered the solemn music and I stopped. I was sort of ashamed of myself to be laughing at Illy-Elly, now that he was dead. Then I thought of his grinning, freckled face and I realized Illy-Elly wouldn't have minded. If he had lived to be eighty I reckon he wouldn't have minded if people laughed when they thought of him. Illy-Elly wanted everybody to be happy.

Grandma came home from the funeral alone. I met her at the front gate. "Where's Grandpa?" I asked.

"He's goin' to make a few calls before supper," Grandma said. She shook her head and made a clucking sound. "Goodness, it's terrible to know there are so many sick children in the community. I was talkin' to Miz Baxter at the funeral. She's afraid that Willie is gettin' sick, too."

"Slow fever?" I asked.

Grandma nodded. "Slow fever." Then she noticed I didn't have a coat on. "Land sakes," she said, "do go in the house this very minute. You'll catch your death without a wrap!"

It was about dark when Grandpa came home. I was sitting in the kitchen with Grandma. Grandpa looked tired. He didn't grin like he usually did, but he went over to the sink and started washing his hands.

"How are the children?" Grandma asked.

Grandpa had a little worried frown. "Some of them seem to be gettin' along all right," he said, "but others are feelin' pretty low." Grandma handed him a towel and he began to dry his hands. "You know," he said, "if this keeps up, we'll have a regular epidemic. I think maybe we'd best be preparin' to take steps if necessary."

140

That surprised me. "What . . . what steps, Grandpa?"

Grandpa shook his head. "I don't rightly know, son—but I think one big help might be to close down the school if things get any worse." He mused a moment. "I guess I'd best try to get with Young Doc Harris and get his advice. That is, if I can find him. He's bound to be pretty busy."

Grandpa was right about that. Young Doc was busier than he had ever been. The next morning we heard that little Effie Meyers and Junior Hamilton were sick. By nightfall, Agnes Ware was in bed. Grandpa's face was serious when he sat down to supper. "It's a regular epidemic," he said. "I've notified the school board to meet with me at the schoolhouse tomorrow night. I've passed the word aroun' that we'd like to have Young Doc Harris there. I hope he can make it."

We ate in silence for a few minutes, then I asked, "What's causing the epidemic, Grandpa?" Grandpa sighed and shook his head. "I only wish I knew, son." He hesitated a moment. "I would have an idea, 'cept that you got sick even before school started."

"What idea, Grandpa?"

Before Grandpa could answer, Grandma spoke up. "I do declare, I think it just floats aroun' in the air. I remember when I was a girl—before the war, it was —they had a diphtheria epidemic up in Millville. All the folks with small children started leavin' town. Quite a few wagonloads had passed through heah before my Papa and the other men in Walesburg got their guns and put up a road block down by the junction. Every time a wagon would come down the road from Millville, they would heist their guns and wave it back. I remember to this day how some of those poor mothers cried and begged to be let through. The men of Walesburg wouldn't hear of it. It seemed a cruel thing to do, but the men of Walesburg thought it would save us from the epidemic."

"Did it, Grandma?" I asked.

Grandma shook her head. "No, son, that's when I lost mah sister Ada. She would have been two years older than I am."

"But, Harriet," Grandpa said, "typhoid is different from diphtheria. It's usually . . ."

Grandma shook her head firmly. "Mister Gray," she said, "I do believe that diseases like that just float through the air. You remember the time they had that epidemic of cholera up in Birmingham. Folks even burned their homes to try to stop it from spreadin'. Mercy knows, it didn't do one whit o' good. It almost wiped out the town, even before it got built."

Grandpa seemed to think that over. "I believe . . ." There was a knock at the door. We looked at each other in surprise. Grandpa got up and opened the door. It was Thad Clements. He lived out near the schoolhouse. His voice was low and hoarse. "Ah came 'round to the back because Ah saw yore light back heah, Parson. Ah wonder could you come with me. That little girl o' mine is . . . is . . . is dying."

Grandpa's voice was low. "Come in, Thad, while I get mah hat."

"No thankee, Parson," said Thad. "Ah'll jest wait eff'n you'll hurry."

While Grandpa went to get his hat, Grandma walked to the door. "Mister Clements, is there anything we can do?"

When Thad answered his voice seemed all choked. "No'm, Ah reckon not—less'n you pray for us."

After Grandpa and Thad had left, Grandma and I sat down and waited. We heard the old clock strike seven . . . then eight—and nine. We didn't do much talking, but I guess we did a lot of thinking. When the clock chimed ten, Grandma looked up.

"It's 'way past your bedtime. Don't you think you'd best go to bed, son?"

"Aw, Grandma," I said, "can't I wait for Grandpa?"

She sighed. "I guess it won't hurt—just this one night."

We didn't have long to wait after that, anyway. Pretty soon we heard Grandpa's footsteps on the front veranda. When he came in his face was tired and drawn. He sat down heavily. We looked at him questioningly. He nodded. "She's dead. She died an hour ago—a pretty, golden-haired nine-year-old girl. The funeral will be tomorrow afternoon."

Grandma clucked softly. "It's awful," she said.

Grandpa sighed and I could see something else was bothering him. Finally he spoke. "I . . . I ran into Doctor Harris over there tonight."

We didn't say anything. We just waited.

143

"He almost snarled at me," Grandpa said, and the recollection made him shake his head with wonder. "He met me on the veranda as I was goin' in. We were both goin' in—an' . . . an' he turned and said, 'Haven't you done enough damage?' I was jest taken back for a minute. 'What do you mean?' I asked."

"What on earth—what did he say?" Grandma asked.

Grandpa's voice sounded almost shocked when he repeated it. "He said . . . he said, 'Mister Gray—'" and here Grandpa's voice sounded dry and precise like Young Doc's—"'I've given up trying to tell you what to do. I'm going to leave it up to the other men in this community at the meeting tomorrow night.'"

"What did you say?" Grandma asked.

"I said, 'I was hopin' you knew about the meetin'.' Then I went in the house."

Grandma's eyes were wide. "Mister Gray," she said, "do you think . . ."

Grandpa sighed again deeply and shook his head. "Harriet, I jest don't know—but I do believe, I actually do believe, that man hates me."

XVI

THERE were only two chores that Grandpa disliked. One was conducting funerals and the other was meeting with the school board. Grandpa disliked funerals because he thought they were cruel. Once when he was young and didn't know better, he tried to do something about it. When Old Amos Belsher died, Grandpa held the kind of service he thought was best. He read a short passage from The Scripture, gave a brief, dignified speech, and finished up with a prayer. Old Amos' relatives were shocked and embarrassed. They were used to long, sad orations, mournful prayers and a lot of hymns. They felt that Grandpa hadn't done right by Old Amos.

When Grandpa would recall that he would shake his head and smile ruefully. "I foun' out then, son, that funeral services aren't really held for the dead. They're held for the survivors—an' they want all the trimmin's, even if it tears their hearts out."

Grandpa disliked school-board meetings because he said they usually ended with him on one side and the other members of the board on the other. They disagreed on nearly everything. It put Grandpa out considerably.

One of the biggest arguments I remember was over the lamps we had in the schoolhouse. They were Grandpa's idea. He visited the school one cloudy day and he was surprised to see how dark it was inside. He told the other members of the board about it at the next meeting and he suggested that they buy some lamps. They hemmed and hawed, and as usual Clem McCollough got up and had his say. It was always the same.

"They didn't have no lamps when Ah went to school," he said, "an' Ah reckon what was good enough for me is good enough for the chil'lun nowadays."

Grandpa just sighed and didn't point out, like he sometimes did, that Clem had gone to school fifty years before.

Grandpa turned to Lon Hamilton. "What do you think, Mister Hamilton?"

Lon got to be a member of the school board because he owned the sawmill. The other members liked to have him handy so they could pin him down and make him donate lumber whenever the school needed repairs. Maybe that was one reason Lon was opposed to anything that sounded like improvement.

"Ah don't think it's good for chil'lun's eyes to be a-studyin' by lamplight," he said. "Ah jest don't want to ruin these chil'lun's eyes."

Grandpa thought that was real foolish and he showed it.

"Mister Hamilton," he said, "is it better for them to study by lamplight—or without any light a-tall?"

One by one, the other members of the board offered objections. Grandpa finally settled the question by buying the lamps himself. When he needed coal oil he would just go by Clem McCollough's store and ask for it. For a long time Clem would mutter and sort of fuss around about this, but finally it got to be a habit to give the school oil and Clem didn't seem to mind. Leastways he didn't let on.

Another disagreement came when Grandpa suggested that the school hire a teacher with a college education. Up to that time it didn't matter how much education a teacher had as long as she had a teaching license. Grandpa suggested that they try to get a graduate from Georgia Institute.

Iris Thomas gasped. "Why, Parson," she said, "that's a co-educational school!"

Everybody on the board sort of gulped. That is, all except Old Man Burtis Moore. He had been on the school board even before Grandpa. He was one of the early settlers in Walesburg.

Old Man Moore didn't hear so well and he put one hand behind his ear and leaned forward. "What's that co . . . co, er, co . . . thing?" he asked, sharply.

"It means that men and women attend school together," Grandpa explained.

Old Man Moore settled back disappointed. "Why, they do that right heah."

Iris Thomas made a round O with her mouth. "But . . . but these are *grown* men and women," she said. Grandpa said she said it like Georgia Institute was a den of iniquity.

Lon Hamilton spoke up right away. "Ah ain't in favor of bringin' no short-haired female to teach these heah chil'lun," he said.

That was too much for Grandpa. He rose to his feet. His eyes were cold and his voice was sharp, like when he was frailing evil in church.

"I've been in this community for forty years," he said, "an' if anybody heah thinks I would do anything to harm our children I want him to speak up now."

That settled it. The school board remembered that Grandpa was a preacher. They decided to give a college graduate a chance if they could get her cheap enough. Even Iris Thomas voted agreement, though she sniffed when she did it.

Things like that were always pestering Grandpa when he thought of improvements for the school. Sometimes when he would mention them, Grandma would ask, "Is the school board behind you, Mister Gray?"

Grandpa would shake his head and sigh. Then he would chuckle. "No," he would say, "but I'm behind them—an' I'm pushin'."

Grandpa was glum the night he got ready to go down to the school-board meeting to decide what to do about the slow-fever epidemic. He was quiet and thoughtful at the supper table. Grandma had to speak to him once or twice to get him to pass something. Finally she got exasperated. "Mister Gray," she said, "what on earth are you studyin' about?"

Grandpa looked up in surprise. "Eh?"

Grandma shook her head and clucked. "Land sakes, what on earth are you studyin' about?"

Grandpa grinned. "Harriet," he said, "if you must know—I was thinkin' about Black Tom."

"What on earth . . ." Grandma started.

"I was thinkin' 'bout his loyalty," Grandpa said. He shook his head slowly. "Loyalty like that is hard to find these days."

I knew right off what Grandpa was talking about. Black Tom had been a slave on my great-grandpa's plantation. He looked after Grandma and her sisters and her mother while Great-Grandpa Scott was off fighting the war.

148

When Great-Grandpa Scott came home, his colonel's uniform all torn and faded and the mark of death already on him, Black Tom was the only servant to greet him. All the other slaves had run off. As soon as Colonel Scott got a chance he called Black Tom into his study.

"Sit down, Tom," he said. Black Tom sat down, timidly.

"Tom," Colonel Scott said, "you know that now you're a free man. Ah don't have any money to pay you for your services to mah family. All Ah've got is Confederate money—an' it's not worth the paper it's printed on." Colonel Scott turned to his desk and picked up a piece of paper. "But Tom, Ah do want you to have this. Ah want you to take it—along with my hoss. It's all I can do for you except shake your hand and thank you."

Black Tom looked at the piece of paper Colonel Scott had handed him. It was covered with my great-grandpa's neat, engraved-looking writing. Tom's face was filled with wonder. "Whuss dis say, suh?" he asked.

My great-grandpa took the paper and read aloud: "To whom it may concern: This man, Tom Scott, has been my slave for fifty years. He was born on my plantation and his parents were honorable people. He is honest, faithful and kind. Above all, he is a man. I cannot praise him too highly. He is now a freeman under the law promulgated by President Abraham Lincoln. I shall forever envy anyone who is fortunate enough to secure his services."

While Colonel Scott read, Tom's face was filled

first with wonder, then dismay. By the time Colonel Scott had finished, Tom's eyes were filled with tears.

Colonel Scott folded the paper and handed it to Tom. He took it and thrust it in his pocket. Then he looked at my great-grandfather and his lips quivered. "Don' yo' mine, Cul'nel, suh," he said, "nex' time we'll lick dem Yankees." Then he straightened to his full height.

"Naow, eff'n yo' don' mine, suh, Ah'll go see 'bout hustlin' up some feed for yore hoss. We'll need him fo' the spring plowin'."

I hadn't thought about Black Tom for a long time. I guess Grandma hadn't either. She smiled at Grandpa. "What made you think of that tonight?"

Grandpa's face was sober. "I was jest thinkin' about loyalty," he said. He put his hand on Grandma's for just a moment, then he stood up. "I'd best be gettin' to the schoolhouse." There was a little puzzled line between Grandma's eyes as she watched him go.

There were only the five members of the school board and Young Doc Harris at the meeting that night but before morning nearly everybody in Walesburg knew what had happened. Sometimes when I thought about it later, it almost seemed that I was there myself. I knew the story that well.

When Grandpa arrived at the school house the other board members were there. Usually they made little jokes about sitting on the children's benches, but tonight they were long-faced and serious. Clem McCollough and Burtis Moore greeted Grandpa like they always did, but Iris Thomas held her thin lips tight. It was plain to see that she still hadn't gotten over her last meeting with Grandpa at Ladies' Aid. Grandpa hadn't seen Lon Hamilton since their run-in about Uncle Famous. Lon didn't seem to recall that at all. He was just red-eyed and tired-looking. Grandpa asked him how Junior Hamilton was getting on.

Lon shook his head and he seemed awfully worried. "He ain't feelin' well a-tall, Parson," he said. "Seems to me that boy o' mine is jest gettin' worse every day. We're jest all tore up about it out to the house." He pulled out his handkerchief and wiped his red face.

Grandpa sat down at Miss Samuel's desk and called the meeting to order. "I hardly know how to proceed," he said, "until Doctor Harris shows up. I think we'll have to depend on him mostly for a decision about the school."

Iris Thomas spoke up. "What did you have in mind, Parson Gray?"

Grandpa shook his head. "I really don't know, Iris. I thought maybe closin' the school might help. It seems certain that the fever 'pears to be spreadin' from one pupil to the other. I think we ought to try to find out why the fever is spreadin' an' where it comes from—if that is possible."

Lon Hamilton jumped up at that. "Hol' on thar a minnit," he said. "Ah got mah own idees about that, an' Ah'd like to have mah say." His face was flushed. He looked at Grandpa. "Lots of folks may not agree with me, but Ah feel sartin that the niggers around heah has got somethin' to do with this epidemic. Everybuddy knows niggers is the dirtest things thar is. Ah think eff'n we jest kept the niggers outta Walesburg that this thing would disappear jest like that." Lon slapped his hands together with a loud sound.

Grandpa raised his eyebrows but his voice was calm. "Do you have any reason for this idea, Mister Hamilton?" he asked.

Lon shook his head. His face was determined. "Nawsir, Ah haven't got no evidence, but Ah got mah own idees."

Grandpa kept his voice low and steady. "Can you mention any particular instance where you thought a colored person passed on this fever?" he asked.

"Ah shore could eff'n Ah got out an' looked aroun' a little, Ah'll bet," Lon said. "Ah see niggers everwhar Ah go nowadays. They walk the streets a-chewin' an' a-spittin' jes' as smart-aleck as yo' please. Ah say right now hit's high time to do somethin' about these dirty coons." He looked around. Nobody moved or nodded. He looked at Grandpa and then his face got redder. "Anyway," he finished a little lamely, "everybuddy knows niggers is the dirtiest thing thar is!" He sat down.

Grandpa's voice was dry. "We're glad to get your idea on the cause of the fever, Mister Hamilton. Now I think we'd better see if anybody else has more, er, ah— definite ideas."

Clem McCollough made a little motion with his hand.

"Yes, Clem," Grandpa said.

"Wal, Parson," Clem drawled, "Ah bin thinkin' this thing over at some length the past few days. Ah was jes' wonderin' if anybody had thought to inspect . . ." Clem stopped suddenly. The door to the schoolhouse opened. Every eye turned in that direction.

Young Doc Harris stood in the door. It was easy to see that he was almost worn out. His clothes were dusty and unpressed. A half dozen sleepless nights had caused his eyes to sink back in his head. He stood there a moment, blinking his eyes in the light.

Grandpa called to him, "Come in, Doctor. We've been waitin' for you."

Young Doc came up the aisle slowly. "I can only stay a minute," he said. "I've got five more calls to make tonight." His voice was heavy with weariness. He put his little black bag on a bench and turned and looked at the other members of the board. His eyes seemed to get hostile.

"We won't keep you long, Doctor," Grandpa said. "We only want to ask your advice on some things."

"Ask your questions, Mister Gray," Young Doc said. His lip curled ever so slightly. "You may not like the answers."

Grandpa didn't seem to notice this last remark. "First, Doctor Harris, we'd like to know if we should close down the school."

Young Doc didn't hesitate a moment. "Yes," he said. "At least that will guard against any secondary cause of infection." He was about to go on, but Lon Hamilton interrupted.

"Doc," he said, "don't yo' think we should keep these heah niggers off'n the streets."

Young Doc turned in annoyance and his voice was contemptuous. "What Negroes, Mister Hamilton?"

That flustered Lon. He waved his fat little arms broadly. "Why . . . why, all these heah niggers."

Young Doc's voice was as hard as his eyes. "Mister Hamilton," he said, "I've got a lot of patients who are ill from typhoid and not a single one of them is colored. In fact, with your son ill in the primary stages of typhoid, you're a greater menace to this community than any Negro."

Lon's mouth fell open at this. For a moment it seemed he would choke. Then he started to bluster. "Now, yo' lookit heah," he said, "nobuddy on earth kin say that . . ."

Young Doc cut him short with an impatient gesture. He drew himself up to his full height. "I am saying it, Mister Hamilton. I'm saying you're a menace to the community. You should stay at home where you belong!"

Lon seemed like he wanted to say something but his mouth just opened and closed. The accusation had rocked him on his heels. Young Doc's eyes were as black as coals. His nostrils were flaring in anger.

Everybody was uneasy before his glance and Iris Thomas gave a nervous little laugh. "Doctor Harris, do you expect the epidemic to spread?" she asked.

Young Doc's voice was brutal. "Yes," he snapped. "I expect it to spread. Every child in this school has been exposed to typhoid fever. Some of them are going to die. It may be your child. Right here in this room they were exposed to typhoid. Worse still, some of them have been exposed in their own homes!" Young Doc's own words seemed to whip up his anger. The sleepless nights and the worry didn't help any.

He turned to Grandpa and faced him. "Should I tell them why typhoid is spreading, Mister Gray?"

Grandpa seemed to pale but he looked at Young Doc steadily. His voice was low. "That's what we're heah for, Doctor."

Young Doc turned on his heel. His voice was high. "All right! You want to know—you want to find out. I'll tell you! I'm convinced that one man is responsible for the spread of this disease. I'm convinced that one single man has carried this typhoid. I warned him! I've warned him a dozen times, but he persisted in butting his way into sickrooms and going from home to home!"

Everybody's eyes were wide with wonder. They looked at each other.

Young Doc's voice went on, sharp as a whiplash. "This man had sickness in his own home. He had a communicable disease in his home but he insisted on coming right down to this very room and sitting with every child of school age in town."

Grandpa's voice cut in, low and calm. "That's a serious charge, Doctor."

Young Doc threw up his head like a high-strung horse. "Serious? Serious! Of course it's serious. It's a crime. It's worse than any of those sins you're always preaching about!"

That was too much for Lon Hamilton. "Who is this man?" he asked, blustering like a pouter pigeon. The others sat forward on the edge of their seats.

Something between a sneer and a smile crossed Young Doc's thin face. He turned to Grandpa. "Shall I tell them, Mister Gray?" he asked.

Grandpa looked at Young Doc steadily. He swallowed and cleared his throat. His voice was low and even. "Say your piece," he said.

For a moment it seemed like Young Doc hesitated, then he tightened his jaw and pointed his finger straight at Grandpa. "You're the man, Mister Gray!" he said. His voice was too loud.

Grandpa sat there like Young Doc had slapped his face. At first it seemed that he was going to defend himself. Then he sort of slumped back. It wasn't in the way he sat. It was more in his eyes.

There wasn't a word in that schoolhouse for a full minute. Young Doc put his hand to his head in a tired gesture. He licked at his lips. For a moment it looked as if he were going to tone down, but then Old Man Burtis Moore spoke up. He probably just meant to keep his voice questioningly, but since he was hard of hearing, it boomed out sort of accusingly. "Kin yo' prove that, young feller?" he asked.

The anger came back in Young Doc's eyes. "Of course I can prove it," he said. "This man with his long-tailed coat has carried around enough typhoid to put every person in Walesburg in bed." He turned on Grandpa again. His voice was sarcastic. "You talk about prayer, Mister Gray. Well, all the prayers in the world won't help now as much as one tiny tube of vaccine."

I'm glad I wasn't able to see Grandpa's eyes. They looked pained and tired enough the next day. I guess

Young Doc expected him to fight back. But he didn't.

Grandpa just waited until Young Doc got through, then he rose to his feet. Iris Thomas said later that she had never thought of Grandpa as being an old man until then. His voice was low.

"Are you absolutely sure about your facts, Doctor?"

Young Doc hesitated for the barest second. Then the hard light came back into his eyes. "I'd stake my reputation on it," he snapped.

Grandpa shook his head as if he were dazed. He looked at the other board members and his eyes seemed to be asking for understanding. Iris Thomas and Lon Hamilton answered him with cold stares. Old Man Moore and Clem McCollough just had their mouths open. They didn't know what to say.

Grandpa swallowed and opened his mouth. He seemed about to say something, but he changed his mind. He sighed heavily and rubbed his face with his hand and shook his head. "I'd . . . I'd best be goin' home," he said. There wasn't a sound. Grandpa moved up the aisle slowly. He seemed to be carrying the weight of the world. The people in that schoolhouse let him go without a word. Young Doc was the only one with any expression. He bit reflectively at his bottom lip.

XVII

WHEN I was small, just four or five, I would go into Grandpa's study every night after supper. Grandpa would pick me up and sit me in his lap and reach for his big, old worn Bible. I would snuggle close.

"Les' see," Grandpa would say, as he flipped the pages, "where were we? . . . Where were we? Oh, yes, heah we are—right on the Gospel 'cordin' to St. Mark." Then Grandpa would look down at me. "You ready?" I would nod, and off we'd go.

Sometimes there would be words I didn't understand, and I'd interrupt Grandpa and ask what they meant. That was the way it was the night he read me about how they took Jesus to Golgotha and crucified Him.

"What's crucify?" I asked.

Grandpa stopped reading. "Why, they took Him up on the hill and drove nails in His hands and feet and hung Him on a cross," he said.

"The kind of nails we've got, Grandpa?"

Grandpa nodded. "Yes, son."

I thought that over, wide-eyed with wonder. Then I shuddered. "I bet that hurt!" I said.

Grandpa looked down at me with his little quiet smile. "Yes, son, I reckon it did." Then he shook his head. "But I don't guess that's what hurt Jesus the most."

"What did, Grandpa?"

Grandpa mused a moment. "I reckon the worst hurt was knowin' that His fellow man had turned against Him. I guess the feelin' that He was forsaken."

Grandpa shut the Bibble softly. "You know, the worse things that can be done to people aren't done to their bodies at all. The flesh wounds and the flesh heals —sometimes the spirit never recovers."

I didn't understand that. "How . . . how can you hurt a spirit, Grandpa?"

Grandpa's eyes were serious. "By unkind words— by unkind deeds, son. Jest always try to remember this —words and deeds can be worse weapons than any guns or swords ever forged."

"Don't you *ever* get well when your spirit gets hurt?" I asked.

Grandpa smiled. "It all depends, son. Sometimes you do and sometimes you don't. I reckon, though, everybody is a little better off if they get a few of those wounds."

"Why, Grandpa?"

Grandpa opened the Bible again and settled back before he answered. His voice was soft. "Well, son, scars like that make a mighty good place to store away understandin'."

I thought of that conversation a hundred times the first few days after that school-board meeting. I wanted to mention it, but I just couldn't. Somehow I was tongue-tied and shy around Grandpa. All the words of comfort and understanding I could think of jammed up inside me and left me with a dull ache. I guess it was Grandpa's fault.

He was like a different person. For the first time in my life I guess I didn't understand him. He had plenty of reason for feeling the way he did. On the morning after the meeting he went down to Clem Mc-Collough's to pick up a sack of flour for Grandma and everybody sort of shied away from him. Even Clem McCollough felt uneasy. Maybe Grandpa could have understood that, but on his way home people even crossed the street when they saw him coming. I know that people didn't mean anything by that, but they were just afraid to take chances. Nearly everybody in Walesburg was wearing a bag of asafetida by that time and some of them were even boiling their water. They were almost afraid to even say slow fever.

I knew something was terribly wrong when I saw Grandpa come up the front walk. His footsteps were slow and weary and he looked almost as old as Uncle Famous. He put the sack of flour on the kitchen table and then walked out and sat on the front veranda. He sat there all day long, staring off toward Shades Mountain and not saying a word. Just as darkness started falling, I couldn't stand it any longer. I walked over and stood by his chair. It took a long time for Grandpa to notice me. Finally he looked up. He tried to smile but his eyes were sober. "What is it, son?" he asked.

"I . . . I—er, nothing!" I stammered. I wanted to say something but I couldn't. I just leaned on Grandpa's chair, trying to let him know how I felt. I guess he did. He put his arm around my shoulders.

"Son," he said, "I hope you'll never let your pride get you in trouble." He looked out at the mountains and it was a long time before he spoke again. "I jest felt sure I was right. I wouldn't give in an' now look at all the trouble I've caused."

"That old . . . old Young Doc Harris doesn't know everything!" I said.

Grandpa shook his head slowly. Then he sighed. "He knows medicine, son. He knows his business." That hurt look came into his eyes again. "I should have listened." Then Grandpa looked off into the distance again, and, though I was standing there, he seemed to forget all about me.

I wandered back into the house. I wanted to cry. But I guess I knew even then that tears wouldn't do any good.

The next day was worse. Grandma let me sleep because there wasn't any school and the sun was high before I got downstairs. Grandma was in the kitchen. "Sit down," she said, "an' I'll fix you some breakfast." I looked around, blinking the sleep out of my eyes.

"Where's Grandpa?" I asked. Grandma tried to keep her voice natural. "He's still in bed," she said.

My eyes flew open at that. I had never known Grandpa to stay in bed so late. He was usually the first one up in our house. "Is he sick?" I asked, surprised.

Grandma bustled around with her pots. "Land sakes, no," she said. "Can't a body stay in bed late once in a while?"

"Don't . . . don't Grandpa feel well?" I asked.

Grandma made a clucking sound. "Land sakes, such a boy. 'Course he feels well. He's just sleepin'. That's all. Now sit down whilst I fix your breakfast!" She stirred around like nothing unusual was taking place, but she didn't fool me one bit.

I sat down quietly, but then I began to think about Grandpa and big tears filled my eyes. I tried to hold them back but I couldn't. Pretty soon I had to sniff and Grandma heard me. There was a long silence. I knew she was looking at me, but I wouldn't look up.

After a while she came over to me and pulled my head up against her side. She stood there like that, holding me tight, until I quit crying. Her voice was soft. "John—you . . . you aren't to worry about your grandpa. I know how you feel. I feel the same way, but if he knew it he'd just feel worse. Your grandpa and I have been married a long time. You ought to know by now that he'll share anythin' in the world with us—'cept his troubles. He holds to those himself." She hugged me tighter, and her voice was firmer. "Just don't you worry 'bout your grandpa. He's carried some

162

mighty heavy loads in his life, an' he always ends up standin' straight an' unbowed. You mark mah words—he'll do it this time." I wiped my eyes. Grandma let me go suddenly and her voice was natural again. "Land sakes," she said, "you'll have me burn your eggs. Now sit up and eat your breakfast!"

I was just finishing the last of my eggs when Grandpa came into the kitchen. He had circles around his eyes and he looked tired even if he had been in bed so long. His shoulders seemed to sag ever so slightly. He tried to make his voice cheerful. "I reckon I over-slept," he said.

I managed a sort of grin. Grandma didn't look up from the stove. "Don't hurt once in a while, I reckon," she said. Grandpa looked at her and then he looked at me. We didn't fool him one bit. He sat down heavily and sighed.

"Have you heard anything new about the fever?" he asked.

"I'll have your breakfast in a minute," Grandma said.

I saw that pained look creep back into Grandpa's eyes. "What have you heard about the fever, Harriet?" he said.

Grandma turned from the stove. Her voice was light—almost too light. "Oh, the fever. Well, Miz Shel-ton stopped by this mornin' to leave me a dozen eggs—she says that Lon Hamilton's boy is a little worse but everybody else seems to be improvin'."

I could see Grandpa relax at this. "Any new cases?" he asked.

For just the shortest time Grandma paused. Then she turned around and she didn't try to pretend any longer. "Yes, Mister Gray," she said, "there are three more cases. One of them is Faith Samuels. She had to go to bed night 'fore last."

I saw Grandpa flinch. He seemed to feel a real pain. It was a long time before he spoke. "How . . . how is Faith?" he asked.

Grandma sighed. "She's not well at all, Mister Gray. She seems to have it real bad." Then Grandma spoke hastily, " 'Course it's much too soon to tell anything. I'm sure she'll be all right. I'm jest sure she'll be up in no time at all."

Grandpa didn't seem to hear this last. He just sat, staring into space. When he spoke his voice was low. "Don't bother to fix me breakfast, Harriet. I'll jest have a cup of coffee."

Grandma almost dropped a dish from surprise. Then her face sort of melted and I thought she was going to cry. The look didn't last long though. She clamped her lips tight, and when she spoke she sounded provoked. "Mister Gray," she said firmly, "I'm goin' to fix you sidemeat, eggs, grits and biscuits. You'll eat them every last speck—if I have to hold your nose."

While Grandpa ate I walked out to the front veranda and sat on the stoop. After a while I heard him walk through the hall and go into his study. I heard him open his desk and then after a short pause there was a low scratching sound. That surprised me. I wondered what Grandpa was writing. He never used a pen unless he was writing a letter. I didn't have to wonder long.

Pretty soon Grandpa came to the front door and I looked up. He held out a piece of paper in his hand. "John," he said, "I want you to take this up to the church and tack it on the front door. You'll find some tacks already there."

"What . . . what is it, Grandpa?"

He handed me the paper. In his neat hand, he had written: "Notice: Services will not be held at this church until further notice. We ask your prayers for the sick." It was signed: "J. D. Gray, Pastor."

I was bewildered. "But . . . but Grandpa, I didn't know you could ever close a church."

At first I didn't think Grandpa heard me. He walked over to his old rocker and sat down and looked off toward the mountains. Then I heard his voice, real low, "You can," he said, "if you know nobody's comin'. People make a church—not the four walls and a steeple."

XVIII

WHEN Grandpa closed the church, it seemed he also locked the door to himself. He was quiet and moody around the house and he spent most of his time on the veranda, just sitting. He slept late in the mornings, and Grandma and I both knew it was just his way of post-poning the beginning of another dreary day. About the only time he spoke was to ask about the epidemic. At first, Grandma tried to keep him from hearing about new cases. She finally realized it was no use. Twice a day, every morning and every afternoon, she would put on her bonnet and walk down to Clem McCollough's store to find out who else was sick or who was well.

Sometimes she told Grandpa about Young Doc Harris, too. It was hard to keep from talking about him during those days. It reminded me of what Grandpa once said about tragedy. He said that the only good thing about it was that it gave birth to heroes. I guess Young Doc was the hero of that epidemic.

He worked night and day. Folks looked at his drawn face and red eyes and marveled that he was able to keep going. Night after night, day after day, he kept riding from one house to another. He stood grim-faced in the light of a dozen lamps and sponged down feverish little bodies. When the crisis came in a case, he stayed until it was over. Sometimes he lost a fight, but more often he won. In either case he didn't show emotion, except maybe to become more snappish. Folks in Walesburg weren't used to being shoved around, but they took it from Young Doc. It was like John Beggs said when someone mentioned Young Doc's bad temper. "It is bad," agreed John, "but even if he wanted to cuss me Ah'd take it. Ah'd take anything from that man after Ah saw him work over mah kid for four hours one night jest to break her fever one degree. Ah reckon he's bad-tempered—but he's good-hearted."

Young Doc took a lot, all right, but finally even he had to break. He had been snatching all the sleep he could in his buggy while traveling from one house to another. Then one cloudy night Young Doc just disappeared. Lights were kept burning all night in half a dozen homes as people kept an anxious watch for him— but he never came by. Frantic parents came knocking on the door of his home, but only Old Black Bessie, his housekeeper, was there. She was frightened. "Ah don't know whar Young Doctor is," she said. "He lef' heah early las' night to make his calls. He ain't come home yit." Her eyes were wide with worry. "Ah tell yo', dat pore man done 'bout wore hisself out. Ah wouldn't be su'prised if he done passed out somewhar."

All over town people gathered to talk about Young Doc's disappearance. As usual, the biggest group was down at Clem McCollough's store. The men stood around talking and trying to figure out what might have happened. Once somebody suggested that Young Doc might have got so tired that he just went off to rest somewhere. There was a lot of head-shaking at that. It was, as Old Clem said, "That jest couldn't be true. When Young Doc takes a case—he hangs on. He stays on that case until a patient dies or gets well. No, Young Doc ain't the kind to go off without tellin' somebody."

Late in the afternoon some of the men were even talking about organizing a searching party when Harlow Hankins came rushing in the store.

"I jest saw Young Doc's rig pull up in front of his house!" he said.

Everybody in that store went rushing out. It was Young Doc, all right, and there was somebody in the buggy with him. When the men got closer they saw it was Chloroform Wiggins. He was driving, and when he saw so many people looking at him he started grinning and pulling on the reins like he was handling a circus wagon. It was plain to see Chloroform was about to burst with pride. Young Doc just sat there silently until Chloroform had hitched up the rig. His clothes were wrinkled, but for the first time in days he seemed to be rested. He didn't even glance at the crowd. He sat there until Chloroform came around to his side of the buggy and started helping him down. Everybody got wide-eyed then, because they saw Young Doc was barefooted and he could hardly walk.

The crowd stood silent until Young Doc hobbled into the house, then it turned on the still grinning Chloroform. "What happened? Where's he been?" a half dozen voices asked.

Chloroform was pleased at all the commotion. "He's bin sleepin' at mah house," he said. "Y'all know that leetle patch o' winter wheat Ah got—wal, las' night Ah heered a noise out thar an' Ah eased to the door an' looked out. This rig was in mah winter wheat an' this ole hoss was chompin' away like he hadn't et in a week. Ah walked out an' foun' Young Doc stretched out in the buggy. He was outta this world. At first Ah was a-feered he was daid.

"Ah tried to wake him up—an' when Ah couldn't Ah jest toted him in the house an' put him on mah bed. Then Ah saw he weren't hurt none—he was jest soun' asleep. Ah jest couldn't wake him up—hard as Ah tried."

"What's wrong with his feet?" somebody asked.

"Ah reckon that's mah fault," Chloroform said. "When Ah seen Ah couldn't wake him up, Ah decided Ah might as well try to make him comfortable. Ah started untyin' his shoes an' when Ah got them off his feet started swellin' up like sausages. Ah hain't never seen nothin' like hit in mah whole life." Chloroform shook his head and clucked. "Yessuh, that Young Doc must not have had his shoes off in a week or two. When

169

Ah took his socks off, hit seemed like Ah was goin' to peel the soles of his feet right off with them. Ah jest ain't never seen such feet."

"What'd you do?" somebody asked.

Chloroform's face was solemn. "Wal, Ah jest het some water on mah stove an' tried to soak 'em down a leetle. Ah reckon hit helped a mite. Anyway, they looked better. Then Ah jest sat there an' waited. Coupla hours ago Young Doc rolled over an' looked up at me. 'Where am Ah?' he wanted to know. Wal, Ah tole him an' he got up an' drank some coffee. Now he's gittin' on some clean cloes an' some bigger shoes an' he gonna start makin' his calls agin."

Then Chloroform grinned and puffed out his chest. "Young Doc done hired me, yessuh, Young Doc done asked me to drive fer him. He kin sleep whilst Ah drive. Ah'm workin' fer Young Doc."

Perry Lokey spoke up. "What's he payin' you, Chloroform?"

Chloroform looked surprised. "Why, we ain't talked 'bout money," he said. "Ah reckon Ah wouldn't charge Young Doc nothin'—seein' as how all the good he's a-doin'."

Chloroform and Young Doc and that old rig became a familiar sight after that. I saw them pass the house dozens of times. Chloroform would be driving carefully and sitting up straight, while Young Doc was sound asleep, his long, lanky frame almost bent double. It was an odd combination, but Walesburgh was proud of it.

Even Lon Hamilton praised Young Doc and Chloroform. His son got well so lots of folks thought he shouldn't have any cause for complaint at all. But Lon wasn't made that way. He just had to have somebody to criticize and it usually turned out to be Grandpa. Lon was afraid to go too far but he would get in digs whenever he could.

"Ah ain't a-sayin' the parson ain't a good man," he would say, "but y'gotta remember he was warned by Young Doc and he didn't pay him no heed." Then Lon would stop and lick his lips and look around to see if anyone was ready to defend Grandpa. Sometimes someone would and he'd shut up. If they didn't he'd go on. "Ah reckon the parson's done a lot o' good—but y'gotta remember he's also done a lot o' harm. Now Ah think a man who brings harm to leetle chil'lun should have to pay for it. Ah ain't jest rightly decided in mah mind what we should do to the parson—but he sho' shouldn't git off scot-free."

Most people just ignored Lon. They were afraid to get close to Grandpa, but they knew that anything that he had done was unintentional. They couldn't forget forty years of good work. I think most of them felt sorry for Grandpa.

Maybe Grandpa didn't know this, or maybe this hurt as much as anything else. Whatever the reason, he couldn't be comforted.

Only once did I screw up enough courage to try it. I guess it was pretty clumsy. It was after dinner one day. Grandpa was sitting in his rocker on the veranda, looking off toward the mountain as he always did. I walked over. "Grandpa, if people got the slow fever from you . . . I . . . I guess it was because of me, wasn't it?"

Grandpa turned and looked at me. "What are you drivin' at, son?"

I was embarrassed. "Well . . . well . . . I guess I had to have the fever first, didn't I? You didn't have it. I guess . . . I guess I'm the cause of everybody getting sick." Something about the look in Grandpa's eyes made me stop. He didn't even answer my question. After a while he put his arm around my shoulders and gave me a little squeeze to show he understood. Then his eyes got that far-away look. "I wouldn't mind," he said, "if I hadn't been so stubborn. I don't know what to do."

I stood there looking at him for a few minutes, and then I had to turn away. I went out to the spring house and cried. For a minute Grandpa had reminded me of Bart Hicks. That hurt more than anything. Bart was the first man I had ever seen with such despair in his eyes.

Bart had lived out on Milford Road with his wife and five children. They were a happy family, but one night the house caught fire and everybody was killed, except Bart. I remembered always the way he looked at the funeral. He didn't cry. He just looked dazed. When the neighbors tried to comfort him all Bart could mutter was, "Ah had everything—now Ah ain't got nothing. Ah had everything—now Ah ain't got nothing." He said that over and over again.

Bart didn't live long after that. He just withered away and died. Even at the last he muttered, "Ah had everything—now Ah ain't got nothing." I remembered always what Grandpa said at Bart's funeral. He stood up in front of all those solemn people and he seemed to be smiling a little. "We've come heah," said Grandpa, "to bury the earthly remains of a man who now has everything."

All that week was bad enough for Grandpa, but when Sunday came it was worse. It was a bright clear morning and Grandpa got up early. He put on his pulpit coat and for a while I thought that was going to make him feel better. It didn't. Long about church time he was so fidgety that he couldn't sit still. Grandma and I were sitting in the kitchen and we could hear him walking back and forth in his study. Ever so often, Grandma would stop what she was doing and listen to his footsteps a moment. Then she would shake her head and sigh deeply. I just sat there.

Sunday dinner at our house usually was the biggest occasion of the week. Grandpa always felt good after delivering his sermon and Grandma was chock-full of information that she had picked up from the other women at church. But this Sunday dinner was the worst meal I had ever sat through. Grandma had the table loaded with fried chicken and biscuits and four or five vegetables and a big chocolate cake. But the food might as well have been sawdust. I tried to eat a lot and so did Grandpa, but only because we didn't want to hurt Grandma's feelings.

After dinner Grandpa usually went into the study and stretched out on the big leather sofa and caught a nap. He didn't sleep this Sunday. When I looked in on him, he was stretched out, but his eyes were wide and he was staring at the ceiling.

I walked back to the kitchen. "Can I go out to Aunt Pim's now?" I asked Grandma.

Grandma seemed shocked. "Land sakes, no. You've just got out of bed, an' I'm not goin' to have you have a relapse."

"Aw, Grandma," I pleaded, "can't I go just for a little while?"

"No!" said Grandma. The way she said it showed she meant it.

I wandered out to the back veranda and sat there a long time. Then I had an idea. I went back to the kitchen. "Grandma, can I go out to Uncle Famous' a while. It's not far—can't I, Grandma—can't I, please?"

Grandma seemed about to say no, but then she paused a moment and nodded. "Yes, I reckon that's all right. But—mind you now—don't stay long and don't get your feet wet anywhere along the way."

I promised and ran out of the house, not taking a chance on her changing her mind.

I found Uncle Famous on the front porch of his little house. When I saw him I felt better than I had in days.

"Why, chile, come in dis house." Uncle Famous said. "Ah ain't seed yo' in so long Ah was 'bout a-feered yo' done gone an' forgit me." His face was covered with a big grin.

Uncle Famous got a bowl of cooking pears and he got out his old bone-handled clasp knife and peeled me one while I told him the story of the slow fever and

Grandpa's troubles. He didn't say a word. Finally he handed me the pear and cleaned his knife. I had almost eaten it before he grunted and then spoke.

"Lawd! Lawd! Yore grandpa sho' haf got him a peck o' trouble." He nodded slowly. "Yes, sah, Ah heered 'bout it, but Ah didn't happen t' think hit was nowhar as bad as hit is."

"What . . . what do you think'll finally happen, Uncle Famous?"

Uncle Famous shook his white head. "Ah don't know, chile. Ah sho' jes' don't know—but Ah knows dat yo' Grandpa will make things turn out all right somehow. Yes, sah, yo' grandpa hain't the kinda man to give up so easy. 'Course he's jes' like everybuddy else; he kinda takes things hard now an' den—but he ain't gonna stay down long. No, sah—dat man jes' ain't like dat."

I sighed. "I guess Young Doc just don't like Grandpa anyway. Even if Grandpa hadn't spread the slow fever, I guess he might have said he did."

Uncle Famous clucked. "Now, chile, don't yo' go puttin' mean thoughts in that haid. Ah reckon Young Mister Doctor Harris is natch'ly kinda high-strung and peevish, but Ah reckon he does a lotta good too." Uncle Famous chuckled. "Hit sho' is a good thing dat man's a doctor, though. Eff'n he was a storekeeper, Ah reckon he'd plumb run all his customers away. Yes, sah, Ah figger he's got one of the sharpest tongues in dis heah town. That man sho' kin get riled up rat easy."

Uncle Famous sat there smiling a minute, then he looked down at me. I had thrown the pear core away and was licking my fingers. "Dat pear make yo' thirsty?" he asked. "Yo' wanta git a drink o' water?"

I nodded. Then I thought of something. I shook my head quickly.

Uncle Famous looked at me closely. He grinned. "Whuss dat mean? Furst yo' say yes, an' den yo' say no. Don't yo' like mah water?"

"Oh, yes," I said. "It's just . . . it's just . . ."

Uncle Famous cocked his head to one side. "What is hit, chile?"

I didn't know what to say. I stammered. "Well . . . it's just . . . it's just that I remembered Grandpa said something when I got the slow fever. He said . . . he said that I must have got the slow fever because I drank some water when I was with you."

Uncle Famous was so shocked that he sputtered. "Yo' . . . yo' grandpa say dat? Hit don't seem like Parson Gray'd say dat 'bout mah water. Why, Ah got one o' the deepest wells in dis county. Mah water's pure as a baby's breaf." He looked at me closely. "Jes' what did yo' grandpa say?"

I was red-faced and awfully embarrassed. I hung my head. "Grandpa said I must have drunk some water when I went fishing with you."

Uncle Famous sighed and then he chuckled. "Thass differunt," he said. "Ah thought yo' grandpa said something 'bout mah well." He put his hand on my head. "Yo' grandpa meant he thought yo' musta got some creek water." He chuckled again. .

I grinned and laughed, too. I was relieved. Then Uncle Famous squinted at me. "Yo' didn't go off somewhar whilst we'uns was fishin' and drink some water, did yo'?"

"Oh, no," I said. "I never drank any. I wouldn't want to, anyway. It just didn't look clean. I didn't know it had slow fever in it, though."

Uncle Famous seemed to be satisfied with what I said. He settled back. "Wal, meebe dat ole creek's got slow fever in hit, an' meebe hit ain't. Ah don't know. Hit's hard to tell. Ah've seed water jes' as clean an' pure lookin' as anythin' give people de slow fever. Sometimes hit jes' gits in a well—'spite of everything."

I sat up wide-eyed. "You mean . . . can you get slow fever from a well?"

Uncle Famous chuckled at my surprise. " 'Course yo' kin," he said. "When Ah furst heered 'bout dat slow fever in town, Ah thought to mahself right off that schule well was done dizeased." He coughed a little and lowered his voice. " 'Course dat was 'fore Ah heered 'bout yo' grandpa."

I sat there for a long minute. My heart was pounding. "Maybe that well *was* the cause of it," I said. It sounded so simple I was flabbergasted.

Uncle Famous shook his head. "No, Ah reckon not," he said. "Yo' kin bet dey checked dat well furst thing."

I still had that breathless feeling. "No, they didn't," I said.

Uncle Famous put his head closer. "Ah reckon dey did, an' yo' didn't know 'bout hit?"

I shook my head. "No, they didn't!"

Uncle Famous started to say something else, but I was already to my feet. I was half-way across the yard before I realized he was calling.

"Whus ailin' yo', chile? Why you' a-runnin' off like dat?"

I turned quickly. "Thanks for the pear, Uncle Famous," I shouted. "I had a good time." Then I turned —and ran.

I was breathless when I got home. I ran up the back steps two at a time. The minute I hit the back veranda I started yelling: "Grandpa! Grandpa!"

Grandpa and Grandma both met me in the hallway. They looked alarmed. I had to stand there a minute and catch my breath before I could talk.

"Grandpa," I said, "maybe the school well gave everybody the slow fever!"

Grandpa's face fell and he sighed. Grandma said, "Land sakes." For a long time there was a pained look on Grandpa's face and when he spoke his voice was heavy. "No, son," he said, "I thought of that." He patted me on the head. I felt terrible.

"Anyway," Grandpa said, "remember you got sick even before school started." He turned to walk away.

"But Grandpa," I said, "I drank from that well!"

Grandpa stiffened. He turned around. His voice was almost shaking. "*You* drank from that well, son?"

I nodded and swallowed. "Yes, sir!"

Grandpa looked at me carefully. There was almost disbelief on his face. "When did you drink from the well, son?"

"Why, when we went out to inspect the roof," I

178

said. "I went out and drank whilst you were talking to Miss Samuels." For a second I thought Grandpa was going to fall over. Then he turned to Grandma. She was looking at him open-mouthed. For the first time in days, Grandpa's voice sounded firm. "Fetch me a fruit jar with a top on it, Harriet," he said. "I'll get mah hat."

Grandma hurried back from the kitchen with a fruit jar. We walked out to the front door with Grandpa. I started to go with him but he shook his head. "No, son," he said, "you stay heah with your grandma." Then he started across the porch. He was almost to the steps when he turned. "Harriet," he said, and he sounded like he did before the trouble, "pack mah bag. I'm takin' the 5:10 to Memphis."

XIX

GRANDMA used to say she never realized how big our house was until Grandpa took a trip. Grandpa was never away much, except maybe to go to Conference once a year or to be guest preacher at a revival meeting, but no matter how short a time he was gone, it always seemed long.

"I do declare," Grandma would say, "it's uncanny how one man can fill a house so full." She would look at me and shake her head. "You and I just seem to rattle 'round like two lost kittens in a barn when we're heah alone."

The night after Grandpa left for Memphis was worse than it had ever been. Maybe it was because Grandpa left so quickly. Grandma had his valise packed when he came back from the schoolhouse with a fruit jar full of water from the well. He had only twenty minutes to catch his train. He spent most of the time changing his clothes. Almost before we knew it, Grandpa was gone.

Grandpa's trips usually were planned far ahead of time. Grandma would pack his valise and every time she would add something she would give him careful instructions. "Now, I've put you in plenty of shirts," she would say, "so there's no need for you to get up and peer at the collars, like you always do, an' decide that you can wear one for the second day. You've got plenty of handkerchiefs, so always put a clean one in your pocket every time you change your pulpit coat." She would pause and think. "An'—oh, yes—I've put in a little package of soda to take in water in case you eat some fruit cake."

Grandpa would look straight at Grandma and nod solemnly. That didn't fool her one bit. "Mister Gray," she would say, "you're lookin' an' noddin'—but you're not hearin' a word I'm sayin'. *Mister Gray!*"

Grandpa would give a little start, then he would grin. "Yes, Harriet, I'll do jest exactly as you say."

Grandma would sniff. "I do declare—I jest don't know." She would turn back to Grandpa's bulging valise. "Now you've got more than enough socks, an' I want you to hang your . . ."

That went on and on. Sometimes Grandpa would look at me and chuckle. "Son, I've often wondered how I knew when to change mah clothes 'fore I married your

Grandma." He winked at me and turned to Grandma. His voice was casual. "Harriet, did you pack mah socks?"

Grandma wheeled around, open-mouthed with surprise. She clucked and shook her head. "I've told you a dozen times they . . ."

She stopped when she saw our grinning faces. She held her lips tight for a second and then she giggled. "Well, anyway," she said, as she turned back to packing, "I do have to tell you where every single thing is. You couldn't find your head if it wasn't tied on."

I guess Grandma was remembering things like that when we sat down to supper on the night after Grandpa left. Her face was thoughtful and she didn't talk, except to ask me if I wanted more biscuits or another glass of buttermilk. There were a dozen questions on the tip of my tongue, but I knew it wasn't the time for them.

I got a chance later, when we were sitting in the parlor. Grandma was tatting and I had been leafing through a copy of Campbell's *Pleasures of Hope*.

"Grandma, when do you suppose Grandpa will be back?" I asked.

Grandma sighed. "Day after tomorrow mornin', I hope."

"Will he know then whether the school well caused people to get the slow fever?"

"Yes, son."

I thought a moment and then shook my head. "I don't see how anybody can tell by looking at that water. It looked clear to me."

"It's not the way it looks, son," Grandma said. "It's what it has in it. Your grandpa will take it to a laboratory and have it examined."

"How will they tell at the laboratory, Grandma?"

Grandma stopped tatting and looked at me. "I don't know the exact details, son, but they'll put the water under a microscope an' look at it, I guess."

"Then they'll be able to tell?"

Grandma nodded. "Yes, son."

"Do you think . . ." I stopped. The old clock started chiming. I counted the strokes—six . . . seven . . . eight.

Grandma looked at me and I looked at her. I knew what that meant. I sighed and got up and put *Pleasures of Hope* in the bookcase. I went over to Grandma. "Are you coming to bed soon, too?"

Grandma nodded. I kissed her on the cheek. " 'Night."

" 'Night, son," Grandma said.

I was almost to the stairs when Grandma spoke. "John."

"Yes ma'am."

Grandma had stopped tatting. In the little island of light cast by the lamp I could see that she was smiling softly.

"Remember, I told you—you're not to worry 'bout your grandpa," she said.

I nodded. "Yes, ma'am."

Grandma threw me a kiss and I went upstairs to bed.

I was up early the next morning. I dressed quickly

and went down to the kitchen. Grandma was making crab-apple jelly. She stopped long enough to fix my breakfast, and she gave me the mixing spoon to lick while I ate my biscuits. I sopped up the tart, still-warm jelly. It was so good, I asked for more.

Grandma shook her head. "You've had enough this mornin'," she said, "but I'll let you pour the paraffin if you want to help."

I liked that. I took the big old iron pot off the stove, and while Grandma watched, I carefully poured a little of the hot wax on the top of every glass of jelly. Every time there would be a little sizzling sound. I would hold my nose over the glasses and sniff up the fragrance. Nobody ever had such pleasant smells in their kitchen as Grandma.

After a while all the jelly was done. Grandma gave me a piece of paraffin to chew, and I walked out into the backyard. For a while I tried to catch a bumble-bee in a jar, but it buzzed away. Then I walked around to the side of the house and looked up at a wasp nest under the eaves. I had been watching that wasp nest for a long time. When it got big enough, I was going to take it out to Uncle Famous. He always said that wasp nest made the best sun-perch bait there was.

Finally, I walked around to the front veranda and sat on the stoop. My jaws were tired from chewing the paraffin and I took it out of my mouth. I kneaded it slowly in my fingers and then I began to shape it into little figures. First, I made the head of an elephant, with a long trunk and tusks. I was busy making a six gun

184

when I heard somebody running a stick along our picket fence. I looked up.

It was Junior Hamilton and Columbus Hanks. I didn't say anything. I just watched them silently. Junior was about my age. He was a tall, thin boy, but he had heavy jowls and little eyes like his pa. He was always pushing other kids around and bragging about how much money his pa had. I didn't like Junior much, but I had never said anything about it because he had never done anything to me.

I felt sorry for little Columbus Hanks. He was a scrawny boy, and he had wrinkles in his forehead like an old man. He had a chapped place on the side of his mouth and it never seemed to get well summer or winter. That was because he kept poking out his tongue licking the raw place. I never could understand why he played with Junior so much. Junior was always pushing him down or playing jokes on him.

When Junior got even with our gate he spied me. He stood there a second, waiting to see what I would say. I didn't speak. Junior poked out the broom handle he was carrying and ran it back and forth along the pickets in the gate. Rackety-rack-rack, rackety-rack-rack!

I still didn't say anything. Junior put his hands on his hips. "Wha'ca doin' up there?" he said.

I looked down and started making a stock to my paraffin gun. "Nothing."

Junior's voice got louder. "Wha'ca got in yore han'?"

"It's paraffin," I said, "I'm making a gun."

Junior hooted. "Makin' a gun—hah!—makin' a gun! Les see yore ole gun."

I stood up and walked slowly out to the gate. I held out my hand.

Junior's lip curled. "Hah! That ain't no gun. Bet'cha never seen a gun. Mah pa's got a big gun. It's got a barrel long as me! Better not no niggers come foolin' 'round our house!"

Columbus Hanks giggled.

Junior turned to him. "Yo' seen mah pa's gun—hain't yo', Columbus? It's the biggest gun in this heah town."

I didn't say anything. Junior eyed me a minute. "Has yo' ole gran'pa got a gun?"

"He's not old," I said, "and he hasn't got a gun."

"Hah!" Junior snorted. "He ain't got a gun! He ain't got a gun! Reckon yore ole gran'pa's a-scared to shoot a gun."

I could feel my neck getting red. "My grandpa isn't scared of anything. He used to be a soldier. He doesn't need a gun now because he's a preacher."

Junior looked at the house closely. I knew he wanted to see if anybody was watching.

"Hah! Reckon yore ole gran'pa would need a gun eff'n mah pa ever got after him. Reckon he'd need one then!" Junior gave another quick, darting glance toward the veranda. "Reckon eff'n yore ole gran'pa don't quit givin' slow fever t'folks, he'll need a big gun."

I clenched my teeth. My heart was pounding. "My grandpa didn't give anybody the slow fever!"

"Did!"

"Didn't!"

"Did!"

"Didn't!"

Junior eyed me a minute. "Reckon everybody knows yore ole gran'pa did. He give it to me. Ah most likely would have died eff'n Ah hadn't been strong." He turned to Columbus. "Didn't mah ma say that, Columbus?"

Columbus licked at his chapped mouth. Then he swallowed hard and nodded.

Junior looked up at the house quickly. "Whar's yore ole gran'pa?"

"He's in Memphis," I said, "and you quit calling him old."

Junior's little eyes gleamed. He got bolder. "Memphis! Hah! Memphis! Yo' hear that, Columbus? His ole gran'pa's done gone off to Memphis. Reckon he's a-scared to hang 'roun' heah. Yore gran'pa's run off to Mem-phis! Yore gran'pa's run off to Mem-phis!"

"You stop saying that," I said. My stomach was tight and the blood was rushing to my face. I felt hot and cold at the same time.

Junior twisted his face and stuck out his tongue. "Aw—what'll y'do!"

My voice trembled a little. "I'll show you, if you don't quit saying that!"

Junior eyed me up and down. He took his broom-stick and drew a line at his feet. "Les' see yo' step over that line," he said.

I stood still, but I was mad.

Junior waited for a minute, watching me closely.

He puffed out his chest and sneered. "Yore a-scared!"

"Not!"

"Are!"

"Not!"

Junior clenched his teeth. Before I could catch my breath, he reached across the fence and pushed me in the face.

I never did figure out how I got through the gate. Almost before I knew it, Junior and I were rolling over and over on the ground. I couldn't think of anything but shutting his mouth. I was hitting and kicking and squirming. I could hear the rustle of leaves as we rolled on them. I could smell Junior and that even made me mad. Whiff-whap-ugh-ouff! We grunted and panted. Then, suddenly, I saw Junior's face right above me. It was grim and determined. Wham! Something hit me on the head and tinkled into a hundred bright little stars. My eyes filled with tears. Junior pushed his shoulder down against my face. I thought I would smother. For a moment I felt panicky.

Suddenly, I realized my arm was twisted to one side. My elbow was right in line with Junior's ribs. I drew back and, with all my strength, drove my elbow into his side. "Ooof!" Junior grunted and his hold relaxed. For just an instant, I saw his startled face outlined against the sky. Almost without thinking, I drew back and let my right fist fly. Whap! My fist landed right on his nose. My knuckles stung. Junior disappeared.

I scrambled to my feet. It was a second before I realized Junior was still on the ground. He was just sitting there with a surprised, dazed look on his face. He didn't seem to see me or to know that we were fighting.

That didn't last long. Junior shook his head and blood began to trickle out of his nose. Junior put his hand up slowly and felt his upper lip. He took it down and stared at his red fingers. He bent his head and looked down. Blood started spouting on his white blouse. "WA-a-a-a!" Junior let out the loudest squeech I had ever heard. "WA-a-a-a! WA-a-a-a!"

He jumped to his feet and started running down the street, screeching and hollering. Little Columbus ran after him, wide-eyed with fright.

Just then I felt a hand on my shoulder. "Land sakes! Land sakes! John Gray, what on earth have you been doin'!"

I had never seen Grandma so excited. She couldn't seem to make up her mind whether to get mad or cry. "Land sakes!" she said, over and over again. She took me in the kitchen and got a basin of water and a washrag and started cleaning the dirt off my face. There was a big lump above my right eye. I squirmed when she touched it.

She clucked. "Fightin'! Fightin'! To think that you've been fightin'—an' with the Hamilton boy. What on earth will folks say? What will your grandpa say? Now hold still. I jest can't believe it—fightin'!"

Finally Grandma got through washing me. She stepped back and clucked some more. "Jest look at your clothes! I do declare I jest don't know what came over you." She stopped a moment. "What did make you do something like that?"

I hung my head and kicked at the floor with the tip of my shoe. "Nothing."

"Nothin'? Such a boy! Land sakes, I've never in mah whole life . . . John, look at me." Grandma's voice was firm.

I looked up slowly. I had to stick out my bottom lip to keep it from trembling.

"Now, what were you and the Hamilton boy fightin' for?" Grandma asked.

I swallowed hard. "Well . . . he . . . he said Grandpa gave folks the slow fever."

"That's no reason for you to be fightin'," Grandma said. "You've got to be bigger than things like that."

"He . . . he kept calling Grandpa old."

Grandma clucked again. "That's no reason, either. That certainly can't hurt your grandpa or you, either!"

"He . . . he said Grandpa got scared and ran away to Memphis."

"That's no rea . . ." Grandma stopped. "What did you say?"

"He said Grandpa ran away to Memphis because he was scared."

Shock was written all over Grandma's face. "He said *that!*"

"Yes, ma'am."

Grandma stood there silently. Then she pressed her lips in a tight line. She sighed. "Well . . . I . . . I don't—you shouldn't fight!" Grandma leaned closer to me. "Son, what did you hit Junior with?"

"My fist," I said.

Grandma sort of sniffed. "Well, you shouldn't

190

fight!" But then she patted me gently on the head.

We didn't mention the fight any more that day, but it took me quite a while to forget that whack Junior gave me on the head. I had a knot the size of a bantam egg when I got up the next morning. I fingered it gingerly while I ate breakfast. Grandma saw me.

"Well," she said, "I do hope that you see now that it never pays to fight." Her lips were straight, but her eyes were smiling.

I put my hand down quickly. "I didn't start it," I said.

Grandma shook her head. "That doesn't make any difference. Nobody ever wins a fight."

"But . . . what . . . what should I do then?"

Grandma sighed. "Turn the other cheek."

"But, Grandma," I protested, "Junior would have hit me on that side, too."

Grandma giggled in spite of herself. She paused a moment and looked at me. Her eyes were tender. She came over and put her hand on my head lightly. "Son, sometimes it's harder not to fight than it is to fight. I want you to always stan' up for your rights, but never fight because somebody eggs you on. I . . . I guess I want you only to fight for the things you believe in— but don't ever fight because you think it's expected of you. Fight for what you believe in, son—but never fight jest because of pride—even if the drums beat and the bugles blow."

I thought that over for a long time. Grandma went back to the stove. "Grandma, do you suppose I'll ever be a soldier like Grandpa and Daddy?"

For just a second a shadow flickered across Grandma's face. She pressed her lips tight and looked at me. "Land sakes, 'course not! Don't be thinkin' of such things. Now eat your breakfast if you're goin' to meet your grandpa's train."

I ate—but all the time I was wondering how I would look in a uniform.

X X

THE 10:10 from Memphis was late. I walked up and down the dingy depot platform and every second I seemed to get more excited. Ever so often I would walk in the station. "How late is she now, Mister Kirby?"

Jackson Kirby was our station agent. He was a tall, lanky man with a walrus mustache and a big adam's apple. He wore a green eyeshade and black alpaca sleeve protectors. "Wal, le's see . . . le's see," he said. He pulled out his big old railroad watch and took a couple of slow chews on his cud of tobacco while he figured. "Le's see, she passed Millville junction at 9:37—so now she's jest about comin' through Peachblossom tunnel. Now, le's see . . ." He raised his droopy mustache with two fingers and took a quick spit toward the cuspidor. "Ah reckon 'bout now she's puffin' down that grade through the cut—she oughta be in 'bout 10:20."

I tried not to wiggle with impatience whilst Mr. Kirby went through all this.

"Thank you, Mister Kirby."

"Not a-tall, John," he said. "That's what Ah'm heah for." He eyed me a minute. "'Spectin' yo' grandpa home on that train?"

"Yes, sir . . . I hope so."

"Kinda unusual yo' grandpa goin' to Memphis this time o'year, ain't it?"

"Er . . . ah . . . I . . ."

Old Man Kirby smiled. "Ain't none o' mah business, John. Jest curious." He lifted his mustache and spat again. "Sho' would hate to see yo' grandpa get some notion 'bout takin' a call somewhar else. Don't reckon he'll let a little trouble run him off, though. Reckon yo' grandpa ain't made of that kinda stuff." His smile turned into a chuckle. "Ah remember the first night yo' grandpa come to this town. Ah was jest a little squirt, feelin' mah oats an' havin' mah first few drinks o' redeye. Ah never will forget how surprised Ah was when he slapped those pocket cannons down on Jere Higham's bar."

Old Man Kirby slapped his leg and laughed. "Yes, suh, Ah'll never forget it. One o' the Barnes boys was in thar that night. He was a mean 'un—later went off to Ohio and got himself hanged for stabbin' a man. Wal, suh, he didn't let out a peep while yo' grandpa was preachin', but after he left Barnes swaggered over to Jere. 'Didn't know yo' let preachers in heah,' he said. 'Reckon folk'll quit comin' if yo' turn the place into a protracted meetin'.'

"Jere jest looked at him coldly. 'Yo' was closer to him than Ah was—why didn't *yo'* stop him?' "

193

I laughed. "Was . . . ?"

Whooo-whooo!

Mr. Kirby smiled. "Thar's yo' train, John."

I ran out on the platform. It was the Flyer, all right, coming clackety-clack, clackety-clack around the bend. The rails were humming and singing. *Whooo-whooo! Whooo-whooo!* That was the Walesburg blow. My heart was beating fast. Watching a train come in always made chills run up my back.

I stood there breathless while that old engine came hissing in the station, then gave a big sigh and stopped and stood there panting and blowing. I was fairly jumping up and down. A couple of drummers, carrying sample cases, got off the end coach. I waited, but I couldn't see Grandpa anywhere. I swallowed hard. My heart was sinking.

Then it jumped. " 'Lo, son."

I wheeled around. Grandpa was standing behind me. He had got off the first coach. "Grandpa!" I said.

Grandpa chuckled and put his arm around my shoulders and gave me a little squeeze. I looked up. "Was . . . was . . . ?"

Grandpa nodded. "Everything's all right, son—now we've got a lot of work to do."

We walked across the platform and Grandpa put down his valise. "Wait heah, son." He walked in the station. I looked through the window and saw him talking to Jackson Kirby. Old Jackson nodded slowly a couple of times and then his face broke into a big grin. He stuck out his hand to Grandpa. He nodded so fast that his big mustache shook.

194

Grandpa's eyes were bright when he came out of the station. "That's job number one," he said. "Now let's go an' do the next one."

We walked up Main Street quickly and we had gone almost a block before Grandpa realized I was struggling along with his big valise. It was heavy and I was holding it with both hands, and panting and puffing, trying to keep up.

Grandpa chuckled and took the valise. Next we turned up Elm Street, with Grandpa not slacking his pace. There were a dozen questions I wanted to ask, but I knew there would be time later on. When we got to the corner of our block, Grandpa turned right. I knew then that he was headed for Young Doc's. I swallowed hard.

We knew Young Doc was home even before we got to his gate. His rig was in front of the house. Grandpa smiled when he saw Chloroform Wiggins stretched out on the seat, fast asleep. My heart was pounding when we went in Young Doc's front gate. I looked up at Grandpa. His face was calm.

Grandpa twisted the front doorbell and the tinkle seemed to echo all over the house. He put down his valise and we waited. It was only a second before we heard footsteps and the door opened. It was Black Bessie. When she saw Grandpa, she drew back a little and her eyes got wide.

"Is the doctor in, Bessie?" Grandpa asked.

Bessie nodded. "Yes, sah, Parson, he's heah—he's changin' cloes." Bessie hesitated a moment. "Won't . . . won't yo' come in the awfice, Parson?"

195

Grandpa and I went in and took a seat on Young Doc's big leather sofa. I felt uneasy and sat bolt upright and looked wonderingly at Young Doc's diplomas hanging all over the walls. I tried to make my heart quit pounding so hard.

We didn't have to wait long. The door opened quickly and Young Doc came in. I was surprised when I saw how he had changed. He looked ten years older and he had hollows in his cheeks. He had changed clothes and shaved so he was neat, but his eyes were blood-shot and he looked tired.

Grandpa stood up before Young Doc seemed to recognize him. For just an instant, surprise flickered across his face. Then he shut his mouth tight and his eyes got cold.

"Yes?"

"I've come straight from the depot, Doctor," Grandpa said. "I've jest returned from Memphis."

"Well?" Young Doc's voice was still cold.

Grandpa reached in his inside pocket and brought out a pink paper. "I think you'll be interested in this."

Young Doc didn't change expression. He took the paper and glanced at it. Then he must have realized what it was right away because his eyes got wide and they darted back and forth across the paper. For a moment I thought he was going to gasp. His face got pale and intense.

"What . . . what water did you run this test on?"

Grandpa's voice was calm. "The school well, Doctor."

Young Doc couldn't seem to believe what he

heard. He looked back at the sheet. "But . . . what . . . ?"

"I suspected that well," Grandpa said, "so I took a sample of the water to Memphis."

For a moment Young Doc seemed stunned. Then his jaw got tight and his nostrils flared. His face was getting red. There was an edge to his voice. "Why didn't you tell me this sooner?"

Grandpa's voice was level. "I knew I would have to have proof to convince you of anything."

Young Doc's face got redder at that. He lowered his eyes to the paper again. When he looked up again, he seemed to see me for the first time. His voice was precise. "Mister Gray, how does it happen that your grandson got typhoid before school started? His was the first case in town, and after his infection you . . ."

Grandpa cut in. "I didn't learn until day before yesterday that John drank from the well two weeks before school started. He opened the well while we were out at the schoolhouse inspectin' a new roof."

Suddenly Young Doc seemed awfully tired. He shut his eyes for just a second and sat down heavily. He ran his hand over his face. I doubt if he heard what Grandpa said next.

"I've notified Jackson Kirby down at the depot to send his colored helper out to the school to nail down the well. If you want to check on the water, I'm sure that we can open it again."

Young Doc shook his head slowly. "The well . . . of course . . . the well." He gnawed at his bottom lip. "Why didn't I think of that. . . ."

For the first time there was fire in Grandpa's voice. "You didn't think of it, Doctor, because you had too much hate in your heart for me. There wasn't room for anything else—even reason."

That snapped Young Doc up. His lips were tight and his eyes were cold. "You can save your sermons, Mister Gray," he said.

He and Grandpa looked at each other steadily for a moment. Young Doc lowered his eyes first. He put his hand to his head. "That well . . . that blasted well . . . I've been a jackass."

"A jackass has to stay a jackass, Doctor," Grandpa said softly, "a man can be many things—even a saint."

Young Doc snorted. His face was almost purple. "All right, Mister Gray," he said, "I have your report, I suppose now you want a written apology. All right, I'll give you one!"

I expected Grandpa's eyes to flash at that, but they didn't. He shook his head a little sorrowfully. "No, Doctor, I don't want any apologies." He looked straight in Young Doc's angry eyes and his voice was low, almost soft. "I would like for you to forget that I'm a preacher for a minute. I'm a man just as you are. An' because I am a man, I make mistakes because of foolish pride an' stubbornness. You aren't any different, Doctor Harris. For a long time you've been tryin' to deny that. You've always thought of yourself as a doctor—first, last an' always. You've tried to make yourself a machine." Grandpa sighed. "Well, you've proved that you're a man in spite of yourself. If you had been a scientific machine, you wouldn't have let hatred blind you to the most obvious cause of this typhoid epidemic."

Grandpa's voice stayed low, but it had a new firmness. "Yes, Doctor—you're a man, an' you've made a bad mistake. You'll make more, an' you won't have anything to comfort you when you do. I feel sorry for you, Doctor!"

Grandpa turned. "Come, John." He walked out of the office.

I looked back as I walked out the door. Young Doc had his lips pressed tight, but he didn't look mad.

When we got to the front veranda, Grandpa picked up his valise. He took a full breath, as if he hadn't had any fresh air in a long time.

We had turned up our street before I spoke. "Grandpa, aren't you going to make Young Doc tell folks that you didn't spread the slow fever?"

Grandpa put his hand on my shoulder. "No, son, Young Doc will do a better job on his own." He paused a moment and tightened his hand on my shoulder. "You see, all I have at stake is mah reputation—Young Doc has to save his self-respect."

X X I

GRANDPA knew Young Doc better than I did. Maybe it was just that he knew the people of Walesburg. Anyway, he was right. Even before nightfall word had spread about the true cause of the slow fever epidemic. Then people started dropping by the house. Some of them had put on their Sunday clothes, others came straight from the fields and the mills. However they were dressed, there was one thing they all shared. They came quietly, almost shyly, and they were all smiling when they shook Grandpa's hand.

Some of them were honest and blurted out the truth like Justin Gilbert. "Ah didn't know whether to believe what Ah heard or not, Parson," he said, "but Ah reckon Ah did. Anyway, Ah got three little boys an'

Ah couldn't take a chance. Ah'm glad t'know the truth."

Other folks just got red in the face. They tried to stammer out some story that they never did believe Grandpa was responsible for the slow fever. It was plain to see that they were trying to excuse themselves, but Grandpa received them as courteously as he did the rest.

The only people who seemed to provoke him were those who said something about Young Doc. Iris Thomas was like that. "Parson," she said, and she held her thin lips in a straight line, "I don't think we have room for a man who can be so careless with his charges. I do think if he can be so careless about one thing, he can be careless about another."

Grandpa's gaze was level. "Iris, this community owes Doctor Harris a debt it can never pay."

Iris sniffed. "Well! I must say you certainly don't owe him a debt—not after all those things he said about you."

There was the shadow of a frown on Grandpa's face. "Iris, I'm dead certain Doctor Harris never said anything 'bout me that he didn't say to mah face. I only wish I could always count as much on other folks."

Iris got red in the face and after a few minutes she left. Grandpa chuckled as he watched her prim figure march down the front steps and through the two rows of boxwood to the gate. He didn't seem to remember I was standing by his side. He spoke softly. "The funny thing is that she really is happy for me, bless her heart. She's jest got to be meddlin' in something. It's too bad there isn't enough good work to keep her busy." Grandpa glanced down and saw my wide eyes. He cleared his throat, and then he burst out laughing. "You see, son," he said, "the ole devil speaks in all of us—even preachers."

Supper was a happy meal that night. It would have been happier, I guess, if it hadn't been for the knowledge that the slow-fever epidemic was still among us. Whenever the conversation turned to someone being sick, that slow, pained look would spread over Grandpa's face. That made me sad. "Nobody else can get sick out of that well, can they, Grandpa?"

Grandpa shook his head. "No, son, that well's done all the damage it can do." He looked thoughtful for a moment. "It seems strange that so much unhappiness and so much sickness could come from such a little place. I think maybe that it's a lesson everybody should ponder. One bad apple can ruin a barrel. One evil man can ruin a community—even the world, I reckon, if he got a chance.

"Wouldn't it be nice," he went on, "if we could jest go out to the schoolhouse tonight and pour all the sickness back in the well and shut it up tight?" He clucked and shook his head. "Wouldn't it be nice if everybody could recall every harsh, unkind word they've said? Wouldn't it be wonderful if we could jest sort of recall all our mistakes and put them in a big box and slam down the lid forever?"

I looked at Grandma and her eyes were soft like they sometimes were when she listened to Grandpa.

"Maybe it wouldn't be a good thing at all, Mister Gray," she said.

That surprised me. "Why, Grandma?"

She sat still a minute, half smiling. "Well," she said, "people learn a lot by mistakes. I guess that's the only comfort a person can get out of makin' one. It would seem such a shame if a body could jest forget them by puttin' them away somewhere an' nailin' the lid down tight. I'm afraid nobody would be very careful."

Grandpa looked across the table at her and their eyes met. I felt awfully unnecessary.

"You're right, Harriet," Grandpa said. "I guess too many people do that with their mistakes an' errors now. They jest shove them back in an empty part of their mind an' forget them. It reminds me of what the Indians used to say about a conscience. They said the conscience was jest a little square inside you that started whirlin' round when you did something wrong. When it first started turnin' it hurt because the four corners hit against your heart. After a while, though—when you had done something wrong for a number o' times—the corners jest wore down."

I was grinning. I had never heard that story. "What . . . what happens then, Grandpa?"

Grandpa smiled and shook his head. "Nothin', son —nothin' at all. The conscience jest spins an' spins— you can't feel it spinnin' because it's all worn down smooth."

"Could you tell that story in one of your sermons, Grandpa?"

Both Grandpa and Grandma laughed. "I don't think so, son," Grandpa said. "It's too simple. It's so simple that folks might not understan' it." He sighed. "Things get more involved every day. When I was up in Memphis I couldn't get over that laboratory I saw. There were bottles in every shape in the world. That room was three times bigger than mah church an' it was crowded with men in white coats, always measurin', always heatin', always workin'.

"While I sat there I got to thinkin'. If one of those men had walked out of that room, wearin' his white jacket an' carryin' one of those queer bottles, he could bring anybody up short by sayin', 'Heah I have a tonic that will give you eternal life.'"

Grandpa drew his chair closer to the table. His face was serious.

"I can see him," he went on, "jest standin' on a busy street corner. All he'd have to say would be, 'Here's an elixir that promises you life forever!' Can't you jest see the people crowdin' 'round? Can't you jest see them fightin' and beggin' for one drop? Can't you see them shoutin'—'I want to be saved until eternity!' They'd give anything for jest one drop."

Grandpa leaned back and his face was puzzled. "Now take me—I don't have a white jacket. I don't have one of those crooked bottles. I jest stan' on a street corner in mah black suit. Suppose I hold mah Bible up high an' shout: 'Heah I'm givin' away eternal life. Stan' heah an' I'll show you how to live forever—a peaceful, calm, soul-satisfyin' life.' Do you think they would stop?" Grandpa shook his head. "No, they wouldn't stop. They'd wonder what I was doin' on a corner. They'd jest look at me an' say, 'There's a preacher—throw him a penny.'"

Grandpa seemed about to go on, but he looked at our serious faces and he began to chuckle. "I guess I soun' like a preacher."

Grandma grinned. "After all this time, I guess you ought to."

"I guess so," Grandpa chuckled. Then his face got serious again. "You know, Harriet, sometimes I get the feelin' that people are beginnin' to be a little ashamed of religion. They seem to think there is something old-fashioned about it. In this house we wouldn't notice it. Religion is part of our everyday life. It should be because it's mah business. But there's something about religion that seems to make people uneasy nowadays. Some of them even seem to think it makes them a little ridiculous if they say they believe in God an' what he stan's for."

Grandma was scandalized. "What on earth makes you say that?"

"Well, I noticed it on the train goin' up," Grandpa said. "A drummer came in an' sat down with me. He was a jolly, fat man an' we had a real nice talk. He told me about his business an' we felt real friendly-like. After a while he asked me mah business. Well, I said I was a preacher. You should have seen his face fall. He got downright uncomfortable. He started right off to apologizin' for not goin' to church, but he wanted to make it plain that he came from God-fearin' folks. I started once to tell him that I dadblamed didn't care whether he went to church or not. 'Course it wouldn't have done any good. After a while he got up an' excused himself, said he wanted to go up front an' smoke. That really provoked me. When he first sat down, he was puffin' a big black cigar, pretty as you please. I guess he would have been put out considerably if I told him I smoked sometimes mahself."

Grandma giggled. "Why didn't you tell him. He might have given you a cigar an' stayed a while."

"Harriet," said Grandpa, "have *you* ever smoked one of those cigars that drummers are always givin' away?"

We all laughed at that, and then we just sat there quietly, grinning at each other and feeling good all over. Grandpa sighed after a while and stood up. He looked down at us. "It's good to be home again," he said, "an' it's wonderful to have such a family. I reckon I was pretty hard to get along with last week." A tiny little smile touched the corners of his mouth. "There's one good thing about it all. Everybody has to be taught a lesson once in a while. It keeps you from gettin' too tight for your britches."

I giggled at that. "You sure took Young Doc down a button-hole or two," I said.

Grandpa just shook his head. He had that same musing smile. "No, son," he said, "maybe it was mah britches that were gettin' too tight." Then Grandpa left the room.

I opened my mouth to protest, but just then Grandma's hand found mine on the table. I turned to look at her and when I saw her eyes I shut my mouth. I knew then that no matter how I looked at it, no matter who won—everything was all right again.

Grandpa went to his study the next day but I guess he didn't get any work done. All day long people were in and out of the house. None of them stayed long. They just wanted to let Grandpa know that they were with him. Even Old Uncle Famous came, bringing a mess of late sweet corn. He didn't even mention the trouble during the few minutes he sat with Grandpa, but when he started to leave I walked with him as far as the gate. He cut his eyes at me.

"Lawd! Lawd!" he said. "Lookit how dat boy done changed. Other day he was all down in the mouf an' 'bout to give up. Jes' lookit him now." Then he grunted, "Umm-mm humgh!" I grinned and hung my head.

At the gate Uncle Famous put his hand on my head. "Let dat be a lesson to yo', chile. Nawthin' ever gits so bad that hit can't be fixed up wif a leetle huffin' heah an' a leetle puffin' thar. Yo' watch affer yore grandpaw good now—yo' heah?"

I nodded my head and he went shuffling off, grinning and as happy as I was.

There was only one thing to spoil my day. About the middle of the afternoon Mrs. Belsher dropped by to see Grandpa. Mrs. Belsher was a widow and ever since I could remember the teachers at our school had boarded at her house.

She was a plump, gray-haired woman and she looked like mothers look in the pictures. All the school teachers liked her and I guess they had reason to.

Grandpa always said that when a young girl came to board with Mrs. Belsher she didn't have to worry about homesickness. "The only thing they have to worry 'bout is leavin' and gettin' homesick for Mrs. Belsher," he used to say.

When Mrs. Belsher saw Grandpa she shook his hand. "I just wanted to tell you that I'm glad everything is all right again," she said. "I would have been over sooner, except for Faith's sickness. Poor girl! She was distressed to death to hear about the trouble."

"How is Faith, Miz Belsher?" Grandma asked.

Mrs. Belsher's eyes looked troubled. "She's a very sick girl," she said. "Her temperature's been going up a degree a day." She sighed. "Her temperature was 103 when I left."

Grandma gasped and Grandpa looked shocked.

"Oh, that poor Doctor Harris," Mrs. Belsher said. "He stays by her bed constantly. It's just a shame! He makes all those other calls and then he comes by the house and stays until all hours. I just don't know when he gets a chance to sleep. I know some people think otherwise, but Parson, he's . . . he's a good man. And how he does love that girl! If anything happens to her I think we'll just have two people to bury."

Grandpa spoke quietly. "He is a good man."

Mrs. Belsher looked at him gratefully.

She and Grandma chatted a while and then she got up to leave. "Let me hear about Faith," Grandpa said.

Mrs. Belsher nodded. "Oh, I will, Parson!"

After Mrs. Belsher had gone, Grandma rocked quietly for a long time. Then she turned to Grandpa.

"Mister Gray, don't you think, er . . . couldn't you go to see Faith Samuels?"

Grandpa seemed to ponder that a long time. Finally he shook his head. "No," he said, "I won't go jest yet." He looked out the window and when he turned toward the room again his face was grave. "If anything happens . . . if they need me—they'll send for me."

Maybe it was hearing about Miss Samuels' sickness or maybe it was just because the excitement was wearing off, but for some reason I felt bad the rest of the day. It was the kind of feeling I got when Grandpa was so sad. There was nothing I could put my finger on. I just felt all troubled inside.

Grandpa must have felt the same way. When visitors weren't in the house, I could hear him pacing in his study. Once when I went in he was standing looking out the window. He was deep in thought and he didn't hear me as I stood at the door. I watched him for a long time before I turned and went away.

When we sat down to supper Grandpa had the same troubled look. He ate silently and ever so often he would lift his head as if listening for something. Something about his quietness must have affected us all and supper was an almost silent meal.

Finally Grandpa left the table and I excused myself and followed him out to the front veranda. It was a bright night and a full harvest moon looked like a big yellow punkin shining in the sky. We didn't say a word and all we could hear was the chirping of the katydids and the little clattering sounds Grandma made as she washed the dishes in the kitchen.

I don't know how long we sat there, but it must have been an hour. Then, suddenly, down the street I heard a buggy coming. It was coming fast and that surprised me. Even Young Doc Harris never drove that fast. Grandpa heard the sound almost as soon as I did. He sat up in his chair and turned his head so he could hear better. I could see his face in the light from the hallway. It seemed tense.

Somehow, someway, that didn't surprise me any. It was as if we had both been waiting for the hum of those buggy tires all day. I don't know why I knew the buggy was going to stop at our gate. I just did. It was one of those things you can't explain. I was right. The horse came cloppy-clop up fast and suddenly whoever was driving reined up just a little to the right of the gate.

Grandpa and I both stood up and peered into the night. It didn't take but a moment for me to see it was Young Doc Harris' rig. I gave a little start and looked at Grandpa. His face was expectant. "Who is it?" he asked.

"It's . . . it's Young Doc . . ." I started, but I never finished. Somebody jumped out of the buggy and I would have recognized that scrawny figure anywhere. "It's Chloroform Wiggins!" I said.

It was Chloroform. He came hurrying up the front walk. Before he got to the porch he saw us against the light.

"Pawson Gray," he said, "hit's Miss Faith Samuels. She's a-sinkin' fast. They want you to come right away! We gotta make haste!"

I could feel Grandpa tense beside me, but when he spoke his voice was calm.

"I'll get mah hat," he said. He turned to go in the house and then he turned back. This time his voice was low, but I could hear it shake just the slightest bit. "Who sent you, Chloroform?" he asked.

Chloroform seemed surprised. "Why, over to the Belsher's," he said.

"I know. I know," Grandpa said. "But who sent you—did Miz Belsher ask you to come get me?"

Chloroform shook his head. His voice was still surprised. "Why, no, sir," he said. "Young Doc ast you t'come."

I was standing close. I heard what Grandpa said when he turned. It was real low—"Thank you, God."

XXII

MY heart was pounding when Chloroform reined up in front of the Belsher home. Maybe it was because of the ride. Chloroform hadn't spared Young Doc's big bay any on the way over. His heavy breathing was louder than the night sounds. I guess it was the fastest I had ever ridden in a buggy. Then, too, maybe I was nervous about what Grandpa was going to say about my being there. I hadn't even asked if I could come along. I had just crawled up in the buggy. Grandpa didn't seem to notice.

Even when we stopped he didn't look my way. He climbed down from the buggy, and I followed him—afraid to get too close because he might notice and tell me to wait on the porch, and still trying to stay close enough so as not to miss anything. Every room in the Belsher house was lit up. As Grandpa reached the front steps, he threw back his shoulders a little. That made me wonder how many times he had done that, how many times he had walked into a home when death was coming near.

Almost as soon as Grandpa's foot touched the veranda, the front door opened. It was Mrs. Belsher. She was red-eyed and she had a little handkerchief pressed tight to her mouth.

Grandpa took off his broad-brimmed hat. We stepped in the door before she spoke. "Oh, Parson Gray, thank Heaven you've come."

Mrs. Belsher's parlor was full of neighbors. They all stood up when they saw Grandpa. They had that ill-at-ease look that people always get at such times. Grandpa nodded to them quietly. Then he turned to Mrs. Belsher and his voice was hushed.

"Where is Faith?"

Mrs. Belsher didn't answer but gave a little sob and motioned with her head for us to follow her. We went through the hall and up a flight of stairs. As we walked up, all I could hear was the thumping of my heart. My eyes were straight ahead at Grandpa's broad back. I was breathless when we reached the landing. I knew the stairs hadn't made me that way.

At the landing, Mrs. Belsher stopped before the first

door. She put out her hand to open it, but then she seemed to think better of it. She rapped softly. For what seemed like a long time we didn't hear anything. Then there were slow footsteps and the door opened wide. It was Young Doc Harris. For a moment I almost didn't recognize him. He was as stooped as an old man. His hair, which was usually so neat, was down over his forehead. The lines in his face were as deep as the furrows in a field. But his eyes! They almost made me lose my breath. They were deep in his head and they looked dull.

Young Doc looked at us for a long moment. I felt rather than saw him stiffen a little. His voice was the only thing that wasn't changed much. It was dry, though it was edged with weariness. "Oh," he said, "it's you."

Grandpa didn't say a word. He looked directly at Young Doc and waited. I guess it was only a second or two, but it seemed a long, long time.

Young Doc ran his hand over his face. "I'll call you if I need you, Mrs. Belsher," he said. She left with a little sob. Young Doc sort of held on to the door jamb. He seemed to be talking to the floor, rather than Grandpa. "Mister Gray, Faith is dying." When he said "dying" it seemed to be the first time that he realized what the word meant. For one awful moment he clenched his teeth. I thought he wouldn't be able to go on. Then he looked straight in Grandpa's eyes. I had seen that kind of look before. A puppy looked at me like that once after he had been run over by a wagon. It was an almost desperate sort of pleading.

213

"Faith . . . Faith is dying," he repeated, and there was despair in his voice, "—and . . . and there's nothing I can do." He clenched his teeth. "The fever's got to break! It's got to break—you hear!" I felt that if he had the strength, he would have grasped Grandpa's lapels and shook him.

Grandpa's voice was soft. "Easy, son—easy."

The fierce light faded out of Young Doc's eyes. He shook his head and ran his long fingers through his hair. When he spoke again his voice was calmer. "I sent for you, Mister Gray . . . because she would have wanted you to come. She told me that. I've done all I can do. She's dying." I thought he was going to break down.

Grandpa's voice was almost a whisper. "You must have faith, son."

Young Doc looked up quickly. His eyes suddenly were so bright that I thought he was going to shout. For a long time his eyes held Grandpa's and then the light went away again. He clenched his teeth and lowered his head. "Her hands are already cooling," he said.

"I want to say a prayer for Faith," Grandpa said. He stepped around Young Doc and started in the room. Young Doc turned to go with him. Grandpa stopped and shook his head. "No, son," he said quietly, "you wait outside. Once you asked me to leave a sickroom. Now I'm askin' you to leave one."

For a long time Young Doc looked at Grandpa. His jaw was clenched. Grandpa's eyes were steady. I held my breath. Then, suddenly, Young Doc gave a deep sigh and stepped back. Grandpa crossed the threshold and closed the door ever so softly.

Once Grandpa told me that prayers are the only words in the world that can't be spoken too late. "God is always willin' to listen," he said, "no matter where you are, no matter how many people have forsaken you —God will pause to hear you." I thought about that when I saw Grandpa walk into Faith Samuels' room. I thought about it as I saw Young Doc lean wearily against the door a minute and then walk into the hall and start pacing. Back and forth . . . back and forth— with only memories to comfort him. I never knew whether he also had hope.

It was a long time before Grandpa told me all that happened in that room, but I think I felt it at the time.

Grandpa walked in and looked down at Faith for a minute. Her eyes were closed and she looked as if she might have been asleep. There was only her shallow, labored breathing to give a sign that she was so near death.

Then Grandpa got to his knees and like a child he clasped his hands and put them on the side of the bed. Then he prayed. People never remember everything they say at times like that. Grandpa was never able to recall just the exact words he used. But he never forgot what he asked God to do.

Grandpa didn't pray for Faith Samuels at all. He prayed for Young Doc Harris and the community. He prayed for God to bring Young Doc to the altar of religion. He prayed for Young Doc to see the light.

"Father," Grandpa said, "this man is misguided. This man is good. This man has lost his way. Help to show him Your shining light. Help him find his way

215

back to the fold. Surely, his mercy and kindness to his fellow man will always be a credit to Thy name."

It was a long prayer. It was a heartfelt prayer and Grandpa was communing with God alone. He couldn't even hear Young Doc's footsteps in that hall . . . back and forth . . . back and forth. He couldn't even hear his little sighs of pain and despair. He couldn't see the strain on his face, nor could he see that Young Doc for all his lines and care looked like a little boy.

I saw them though—and I know God must have seen them, too. It happened quickly. I felt peace and quiet. I just knew that Grandpa couldn't fail.

And Grandpa, inside, kneeling by the bed, had his sign. Lightly as a falling leaf, he felt Faith Samuels' hand cover his own on the bed. For a minute he didn't notice. Then for one breathless moment he paused. He clasped her hand and looked at her face. It was quiet, unmoved. Then he was shocked to realize that her hand felt clammy. He turned it over. Across that small palm, the lines looked silvery. There was just the faintest, tiniest bit of perspiration. Grandpa shut his eyes tight and thanked God.

I knew something had happened when Grandpa opened the door. Both Young Doc and I pinned our eyes to his face. "Doctor," he said, "I think you should see this."

Young Doc dashed into the room. I looked in and watched as he bent over the bed. Then I heard Young Doc's voice and it sounded young and fresh. "Get Mrs. Belsher!" he said. "Get Mrs. Belsher—and get more water!"

There was a lot of hustle and scurrying around then. I couldn't keep up with it all because it was getting late and even with the excitement I had a hard time staying awake. Grandpa and I went down to the parlor. The people made room for us and we sat down and waited.

Sometime later Mrs. Belsher came in and she was laughing and crying at the same time. "Faith's temperature has broken one point," she said. "She's sleeping."

Grandpa stood up. "I think we'd best be goin'," he said. Then he smiled at me. "John's 'bout to go to sleep."

"Oh, thank you for coming, Parson," Mrs. Belsher said. She dabbed at her eyes. "Oh, thank you."

Grandpa picked up his hat, turned and nodded to everyone, and we started toward the door. Then somebody said, "Wait!"

We turned. It was Young Doc Harris. He still looked tired and worn but his shoulders were straight. Every eye in that room followed him as he walked up to Grandpa. "Mister Gray," he said, "I want to thank you." He held out his hand and Grandpa shook it.

Young Doc bit at his bottom lip and looked down at the floor. We all waited. He seemed to be searching for the right words. Finally he looked at Grandpa. "Mister Gray . . . I . . . I'm a practical man. I don't believe in miracles." He swallowed hard. "But . . . I . . . I do want to say that something—somewhere—saved Faith tonight after I had . . . had given her up." For a moment amazement flickered over his face. He stretched out his long, slender hands and studied them.

Then he raised his face and wonder was in his eyes. "I . . . I didn't save her," he said, "so—so something else did."

There was a long silence, broken only by a little sob from Mrs. Belsher.

Grandpa put out his hand and gently laid it on Young Doc's shoulder. His voice was low and thankful. "Son, when you realize that—you're already half-way to Glory."

XXIII

GRANDPA once told me that nothing was as good a measurer of a man as his memories. "If he remembers all the unhappy, bitter things—then he has to be unhappy an' bitter himself," Grandpa said. "Every person sees in the world an' in other people that which he carries in his own heart."

By that token, I guess Walesburg was a good town. When spring came flooding down our valley, winter retreated swiftly and it carried with it all the unhappiness and bitterness caused by the slow-fever epidemic. A few hearts had a heavier burden of grief and there were four new white markers out at Rehobeth Cemetery, but otherwise our town was unchanged.

It was a wonderful spring. The new corn seemed to burst from the ground, and the fruit trees were thick with blossoms. The air was heavy with the sweetish smell of cape jesamine and honeysuckle. Every morning I was awakened by two sassy blue jays who were building a nest in the water oak outside my window. On my way to school I would stop a dozen times to chase a June bug, to listen to a mockingbird or to gather a handful of honeysuckle and suck the bit of nectar hidden away in the tip of each blossom. Even school was fun that spring. I guess Miss Samuels had a lot to do with it. She was gay and bright-eyed and sometimes she didn't seem like a teacher at all. Everybody in town knew she was promised to Young Doc. She wore his mother's ring on her hand. Sometimes I used to think that I was the only person who wasn't happy because Miss Samuels was going to get married. I think I loved her myself.

But then school was out, and I was beaming and happy like everyone else when I stood in Mrs. Belsher's parlor while Grandpa married Miss Samuels and Young Doc. I had been to lots of weddings, but I must not have listened very closely. That was the first time I realized that a wedding ceremony could be as beautiful as a prayer. I never forgot Miss Saumels' voice as she repeated after Grandpa, "I, Faith, take thee, Randolph, To be my wedded husband; And I do promise and covenant; Before God and these witnesses; To be thy loving and faithful wife; In plenty and in want; In joy and in sorrow; In sickness and in health; as long as we both shall live."

After the wedding, there was a lot of giggling and kissing and Clem McCollough gave out little bags of rice for us to throw at Miss Samuels and Young Doc as they drove away in his rig. Young Doc was red in the face, but he was happy, too. I guess he was surprised to see that he had so many friends.

Grandpa and I walked home in the dusk alone, leaving Grandma behind to chat a minute with Mrs. Belsher. "Grandpa," I said, my eyes still shining at the recollection, "I guess people are awfully happy when they get married—aren't they?"

Grandpa chuckled. "Yes, son."

I sighed. "I guess love must be awfully nice."

Grandpa put his hand on my shoulder. "Even the Garden of Eden wasn't complete without it," he said.

"I . . . I wonder what would have happened if Miss Samuels had died of the slow fever," I said. "I guess it would have changed everything so much that Young Doc would always have been unhappy."

"Yes, son," said Grandpa, "I guess he would have."

"I guess he never would have called you Parson, or started coming to church, either."

Grandpa waited a long time before he answered. His voice was thoughtful. "I don't rightly know, but I don' think that would have made any difference. If Faith had died the result would have been the same."

"But . . . how . . . why . . ."

Grandpa tightened his hand on my shoulder. "It's like this, son—nothin' ever convinces a person of life heahafter as much as standin' by an' seein' a loved one put in a grave. When someone you love dies, you jest know—you jest feel that isn't the end. No, son, sometimes it takes death to bring a man to his knees."

We were silent as we turned in our gate. For ever after I was to remember how I lingered on the veranda and looked up at the moon and smelled the fragrance of that night. Death seemed so far away—and yet it was so close.

The next morning Grandma let me take off my shoes for the first time that year. My feet were tender like they always were in the spring, but I frolicked around like a horse put out to pasture. Then I remembered how cool the creek bank always felt to my feet and how I liked to lie there with a fishing pole and dig my toes into the soft earth.

I hurried in the house. "Grandma, can I go out to Uncle Famous'?"

Grandma smiled. "Fishin'?"

I grinned. "If Uncle Famous wants to."

Grandma sighed and shook her head. "Land sakes, I suppose so. You really do run Uncle Famous ragged when vacation time comes along. Go upstairs an' put on your overalls, an' come back downstairs before you leave. I want to send Famous a loaf of gingerbread."

It took me a long time to get out to Uncle Famous' that day. There were too many things along the way to claim my attention. Out near the Miller place a mother Bob White with a flock of chicks crossed the road almost in front of me. I tried to catch the chicks, but the mother made a clucking sound and they scurried into the bushes, like brown leaves before an autumn wind. I stopped and tried to find them. The mother started floundering and fluttering on the ground like she had a broken wing. I knew it was just her way to try to make me follow her, but I tried to catch her anyway. She led me away from the chicks and disappeared into a blackberry bramble. I searched around for a minute before I heard a sound behind me. I turned just in time to see that the mother had back-tracked and was leading her chicks into a thicket on the other side of the road. I grinned.

Later on I heard the screech of a hawk. I squinted my eyes and looked into the bright sky. I could see it way up high, soaring in long, easy circles. I plucked a blade of Johnson grass and held it between my hands and blew on it. It sounded like a hawk all right, except maybe a little hoarser, but the hawk wouldn't come near.

At the bridge across the little branch in front of Uncle Famous' house, I stopped to watch big, fat tadpoles wiggle around below the watercress. Some of the tadpoles already had hind legs. I knew that it wouldn't be long before they were frogs.

While I stood there, I heard a noise in the bushes behind me. I looked back and a coachwhip as long as my leg came slithering down toward the water. I looked for a rock, but couldn't find one. That snake saw me, but he just came gliding on, with his head held high. I turned and ran.

When I got to Uncle Famous I was still puffing and blowing a little. Uncle Famous was digging in his storm cellar with a long-handled spade. He looked up grinning. "Whuss de mattah, yo' so winded dere, chile? Whuss bin chasin' yo'?"

I told him about the snake.

223

Uncle Famous chuckled. "Dat's ole Tom, dat snake is," he said. "He'll run yo' hips off eff'n yo' go foolin' 'round dat branch dis time o' year. He thinks dat his own pursonnal properitty. He bin livin' dere a long time now. He sho' keeps de mice outta mah fields."

I gave Uncle Famous the gingerbread and his face broke into a big grin. "Yo' grandma makes de most toothsome gingerbread in dis county. Jes' take hit up to mah kitchen an' put hit on the table. We'll have it wif some milk 'fore yo' go."

After I had taken the bread to the house, I asked Uncle Famous if we could go fishing. He shook his head.

"Ain't no use even wettin' a line," he said. He paused a moment and looked up at the sky. "Can't yo' feel dat weather jes' settlin' down 'round yore ears? Dat means dat de fish is gettin' deeper down in de creek. Dey most likely won't be comin' up fo' coupla days. Yes, sah, dis ain't no weather to go fishin'. Dis is almost storm weather. Dis is when de ole cold air an' de ole hot air start a-fightin'. Ah wouldn't be su'prised eff'n we don' git a little blow 'fore even'."

I grinned. "How do you know, Uncle Famous?"

Uncle Famous chuckled and shook his head. "Ah don't know, chile—Ah jes' knows. Hit's a feelin' Ah gits in mah bones."

"Is that why you're digging out your storm cellar, Uncle Famous?"

"Wal," said Uncle Famous, "not eggactly. Ah do dis ever' year. Ah bin doin' dis long as Ah kin 'members." He chuckled. "Don't hurt none, nohow. Ah

224

keeps mah presarves in mah storm cellar." He walked down into the cellar. "Now yo' come on down heah an' sit wif me whilst Ah dig out dis dirt what fell in dis winter."

I sat down on the floor of the cool cellar and watched Uncle Famous dig at the earth with sure strokes. "Uncle Famous," I asked after a while, "do you remember ever being in any storms?"

Uncle Famous paused. "Does Ah 'member? Does Ah 'member? Ah sho' do 'member." His eyes got wide, like they always did when he told me stories. "Why, nearly ever year we has a storm come snortin' 'round heah somewhar. Don't nevah do much damage, but dat don't mean it hain't." He turned and dug some more and then he grunted. "Yes, sah! When storm weather comes 'long, yo' gotta be ready. Ah takes good care of mah storm cellar. Ain't no storm gonna git me. Ah jes' comes out heah an' lays down an' takes hit easy when de weather looks bad."

I didn't put much stock in what Uncle Famous said until I started home that afternoon. The sun was sinking like a big ball of fire, but the sky looked dull and flat. There wasn't even the faintest breeze, and everything was so still and quiet that I could hear the plop of my bare feet against the dust of the road. Once I stopped and looked up at the sky. I couldn't find a single cloud. I didn't think it was going to rain because of that, but I knew it was unusual weather.

It wasn't until I got ready for bed that I thought about the weather again. After I had turned out the lamp, I stood by the open window a long time and looked into the night. It was as dark as the inside of a gopher hole, with not a star in sight. The katydids were quiet. All I could hear was a lone tree frog croaking in the water oak.

I was almost asleep when a faint breeze sprang up and rattled the window blind ever so slightly. I stretched out in the bed and dug a little deeper into the mattress. I smiled. Uncle Famous might be right after all, I thought, it might rain. The bed felt soft . . . and good. I must have gone to sleep still smiling.

Suddenly, it seemed like no time at all, I heard the shutter go bump—bump—bump. I turned a little in annoyance, but the sound wouldn't go away. *Knock-knock-knock!* I shifted again and opened one eye. Then I was wide awake. It wasn't the shutter at all. It was someone knocking on the front door. *Knock-knock-knock!* The sound was loud and urgent.

I was about to call to Grandpa, when I heard the sound of his voice. "I'm comin'," he said. "I'm comin'."

I saw the reflection of his lamp and heard the swish of his carpet slippers as he walked past my door. I jumped out of bed and walked over to the door. Just as I did, Grandma came out of her room. "Who is it?" I asked. Grandma put a finger to her lips and we both cocked our heads toward downstairs.

We heard Grandpa fumble with the front door and then we heard Old Man Tom Abercrombie's voice. It was excited. "Ah hate to git you up at this hour, Parson, but a tornado's done hit out near the Westfield Road section. We're sendin' some help out thar, an' we'd like to borrow some iodine."

I felt Grandma tense and heard her gasp. We looked at each other in shocked surprise.

"Mister Gray," Grandma called, "ask him if he knows whether or not the Scott place was hit."

Old Man Abercrombie heard Grandma. He raised his voice. "Ah don't know, ma'am, but it went right through that section. We ain't got a full report on it yet."

Grandma just said one word—"Pim!" Then she turned and ran back toward her room, taking off her wrapper as she went.

I stood listening long enough to hear Grandpa's voice. "Thank you, Tom. We'll get dressed and get out there right away."

I turned and went to the window. The night was as calm and peaceful as ever. There was only that deep, heavy darkness to make it seem unusual. I was still standing by the window when Grandpa came upstairs and paused by my door.

"Get dressed in haste, son. We'll drive out an' see if your Aunt Pim is all right."

XXIV

THE whole town was awake by the time Grandpa had hitched up old Joshua. I had never seen so many lights shining at night. But what I always remember is the sound. In that quiet night, there was a sort of buzz rising from Walesburg. A hundred voices were raised in surprise, fright or grief. I was scared myself, with an uneasy, excited fright, but when I looked at Grandpa I felt better. In the lantern light, his face was set but calm.

We drove old Joshua around to the front gate and Grandma came hurrying down from the veranda. Her arms were filled with blankets and what medicines we had. She was breathless when Grandpa helped her into the buggy. "I do hope Pim is all right," she said. Grandpa wrapped us both in his old buffalo buggy robes. His voice was calm, "Now, Harriet, don't worry. We'll see."

It wasn't long before we found the first signs of the tornado. Right on the outskirts of town, the Mathis home had been smashed to kindling. Pieces of the roof were scattered in the road and Joshua picked his way around them. Grandpa slowed up for a minute and we strained our eyes into the darkness.

Then we saw the flickering of lanterns and heard the low hum of voices. Help had already arrived. Grandpa slapped his reins across old Joshua's back and we went a little faster with a sort of icy dread.

After that, that familiar old road turned into a nightmare. We passed house after house and it made my heart sink to see them. Some of them had been smashed to pieces. Some had just lost their roofs, and some stood lopsided and pushed to one side. We didn't stop at any of them because we saw lights and we knew someone was up and able to get around.

It was when we got to Carleton Junction that I

shivered. Four houses had stood there. Now they were gone. Even the chimneys were knocked down. Somewhere in the darkness I could hear the wail of a baby. It was a scared, hurt cry.

Someone stood in the middle of the junction, waving a lantern. When we drew abreast of the light, Grandpa reined up Joshua. It was Henry Abernathy. We gasped when we saw his face. It was bloody from a big gash on his forehead. He looked dazed and didn't seem to recognize us.

"Up the road," he said. "Go up the road. They need help!"

"Is there anything we can do heah, Henry?" Grandpa asked.

Henry shook his head. That started the blood spurting down his face again. "We'uns are all right," he said. He wiped his bloody face with his hand. "Ah got nicked with a tin shingle off'n the hen house, but we'uns got in the storm shelter." He stood there a moment shaking his head. His voice was filled with disbelief. "Hit sounded jest like a big ole train, a-roarin' an' a-tootin'. Hit sounded like ole number eight, a-tootin' down the track. When it smacked into our house, hit went boom! like a shotgun. Hit exploded! It didn't blow down, it exploded!"

"Has help already gone up Westfield Road?" Grandpa asked.

Henry didn't seem to hear. He was still thinking about the awfulness of that storm. "Hit exploded!" he said over and over again. "Hit exploded!"

Grandpa clucked to Joshua and we turned up Westfield Road. We were quiet now, filled with our thoughts and a chilled dread. We passed other houses, twisted and torn, but Grandpa didn't even slow up. Once we had to stop because a big oak limb was blocking the road. Grandpa got out and pulled it off to one side. He didn't say a word but climbed back into the buggy and slapped the reins and sent Joshua off in a trot. Even Grandpa's face was tight now. Once he reached over and patted Grandma's hands. She didn't seem to notice. She was staring straight ahead.

I had walked Westfield Road a hundred times, but it never seemed as long as it did that night. I listened to the creak of the buggy and the hum of its wheels on the dirt road, and I made a sort of prayer out of the rhythm. "Protect Aunt Pim," I said. "Protect Aunt Pim."

Finally we passed Lokey Branch and we tried to pierce the darkness by staring hard toward Aunt Pim's house. I saw it first. I breathed a sigh of relief. "It's not hurt," I said excitedly. "It's not hurt!"

Grandpa flicked the reins. Old Joshua broke into a gallop.

We turned into Aunt Pim's drive before I saw that I was mistaken. The whole left side of that big house was smashed and broken. It was easy to see that the tornado had hit it full force. I looked for a moment, with my heart in my throat, and then I gasped. Aunt Pim's tree was gone! Aunt Pim's lovely tree with the sword had been blown down. I could see the outline of its big bulk lying on the ground near the porch. I wanted to cry.

We were almost abreast of the front door before

we saw that there was a light in the parlor. I felt Grandma tense for a moment and then give a little sigh of relief. "Thank Heaven," she said.

Grandma was out of the buggy almost before it stopped rolling. She hurried in the house. I stayed with Grandpa until he had hitched Joshua. All the time I was looking around and the sight scared me. Aunt Pim's big oak had smashed part of the front porch as it fell. Big branches from the tree and pieces of timber from the house cluttered up the front lawn. It was an awful sight. I pressed close to Grandpa. I almost hated to go in the house.

When we got in the parlor, I knew why. Aunt Pim was lying on her big plush sofa and Grandma was bending over her. John Pelham and his wife stood by silently. They lived up the road and they were the first to reach Aunt Pim. Their own house hadn't been hit.

I moved closer to the sofa. Aunt Pim didn't seem to be hurt at all. I couldn't see a mark on her. And she was smiling, smiling quietly as she always did.

Agnes Pelham started crying when she told what had happened. "We got heah as soon's we could. We foun' Miss Pim on the porch. We had to heist up a big limb of that tree to get her out. It had fallen right across her chest."

"Are you hurt bad, Pim?" Grandma asked. "Do you feel any pain?"

Aunt Pim seemed to be trying to talk, but not a word would come. She just lay there, looking small and frail and smiling that quiet smile.

Grandpa stooped and picked her up as easily as he

would have a kitten. Pain flashed across Aunt Pim's face for a second and she gasped. Then she lay quietly while Grandpa carried her upstairs. Grandma scurried ahead to turn the covers down. I sat down while Agnes Pelham went around lighting all the lamps she could find. Then she heated some water and carried it up to Aunt Pim's room.

After that, Grandpa, John and I just sat there in that quiet parlor and waited. We knew it wasn't any use trying to get Young Doc. There were a hundred hurt folks between there and Walesburg. We knew that he would take them as they came, until finally he reached us.

It was a long time before Grandma came downstairs. Her mouth was tight and she had been crying. Grandpa went over and put his arm around her shoulder. "How is she, Harriet?"

Grandma shook her head slowly. "I think she's hurt badly. Her chest seems to be almost crushed." Then Grandma burst into tears. I had to hold my lips tight and swallowed hard to keep from crying with her.

It was a long night. We couldn't do anything but wait—and pray. We did a lot of both. Ever so often Grandpa would tiptoe up the stairs. When he came back, he always said the same thing: "There's no change."

Finally dawn came seeping through the windows and light filled the room. Grandpa and John didn't seem to notice, but I got up and blew out the lamps, and then I stepped out on the front veranda.

The sight of things wrenched at my heart. I knew

that the house would never be the same again. It couldn't be because the tree was gone. Somehow that tree made all the difference.

As I walked down the front steps, I could hear a rooster crowing far off in the distance. Just that familiar sound made me pause. I realized I had heard roosters crow all the mornings of my life. They had crowed on the morning I was born. They would crow on the morning I died. Suddenly, I knew for the first time what Grandpa had meant in one of our talks long ago. "Son," he had said, "we are all pretty self-centered, but we show it most of all when we think about life. When you say life, everyone thinks of his own little life, his own personal little world. Actually life is jest a broad stream. We each ride along on it until we reach separate destinations."

Grandpa had chuckled, like he always did when he thought he was getting too serious. " 'Course I don't mean you jest sit still an' let yourself be pushed along. Sometimes you need help an' sometimes you need a lot of room. But always remember—when the going gets rough, somebody else has passed along there, an' they managed to get through. An' whatever you do, don't try to turn aroun' and start fightin' your way back upstream. You can't do that. You have to go ahead—but jest keep an eye peeled for the shoals ahead."

As I looked at that dawn, I knew what Grandpa meant and I guess I knew that time was the only thing that didn't change. For as long as time, roosters had crowed at dawn. Birds had chirped at dawn—and somewhere people had met a lightening sky with sorrow or

233

happiness in their hearts. Life went on. Sorrow vanished. Sometimes happiness did.

I walked out in the yard slowly and looked at the long, rough length of Aunt Pim's tree. Suddenly, I remembered the sword. Now I could see the sword close up. I could even touch it!

I ran to the trunk, and there it was—a full two feet of sword sticking out from that big tree. Fifty years had dulled its shine and eaten away at its width—but it was intact. I stooped and my hand trembled a little as I ran my hand along its surface. I peered closer in the early morning light—then, I froze with surprise. Something was wrong!

I fingered the blade slowly, and then I knew it wasn't a sword at all. It wasn't even shaped like a sword when you examined it closely. It was a scythe—a plain, ordinary field scythe! My mouth was open with wonder and surprise.

I don't know how long I knelt there before I heard footsteps on the porch. It was Grandpa. He was walking toward me.

"Grandpa," I said, "this isn't . . . this isn't . . ."

Grandpa put his hand on my head. "I know, son. I know."

I couldn't understand. "But, Grandpa, it isn't . . ."

There was a sad little smile on Grandpa's face. "Sit down, son."

I sat down on the old tree trunk, filled with wonder. Grandpa sat next to me.

Grandpa's voice was soft. "It was a wonderful story, wasn't it? It was the sort of story that everybody

234

likes. It had a hero an' a heroine. It had romance an' it had bravery."

"But Grandpa," I said, "it's not true. This isn't a sword!"

Grandpa shook his head slowly. "No, son, it isn't a sword. It's a scythe. Sometime—a long time ago—someone, probably a slave, hung it up in this tree. It was a little tree then, and everybody forgot the scythe, except the tree. It grew aroun' it. It embraced it—an' there it is now, fifty years later."

"But Captain Hall," I said, "—Captain Hall and Aunt Pim?"

Grandpa didn't seem to hear my question. "Your Aunt Pim is a wonderful woman, son. She's a good woman. She's a kind woman. She would have made some man a wonderful wife. But she never married, son—an' I guess she never had a chance.

"At first I guess Pim started tellin' the story in fun. Maybe it was because it was romantic. Maybe it was a story that should have happened." Grandpa sighed and clasped his arm tighter around my shoulder. "Whatever the reason or cause, Pim must have really begun to believe that story. She made it so real that people aroun' her almost began to believe it too. I never heard anyone who knew the truth deny it, an' there aren't many people left now who remember whether it is true or not."

Grandpa looked at me and smiled a little sadly. "You see, son—sometimes when life passes people by, they jest make up dreams to pretend it isn't so."

My lip trembled. "But . . . but it isn't true . . ."

Grandpa didn't say anything for a long time. When

he spoke his voice was soft. "True? . . . True? Of course, it's true, son. It's true because Pim made it that way. All these years she lived that story. Maybe it was an excuse to begin with—but it wasn't an ordinary kind of excuse. Pim didn't need that kind. Yes, son—Pim's story is true . . . it jest isn't real." He smiled softly. "Some day you'll know the difference."

I started crying, softly.

Grandpa tightened his arms. "Don't cry, son. All dreams aren't so beautiful—even when you wake up."

"I wish—I wish I had known," I sobbed.

"No, son," Grandpa said. "Some things are better if you don't know." His voice was almost a whisper. "Ella has a baby. Pim had a tree. Some people don't have anything but empty hopes."

After Grandpa went into the house, I sat on the tree trunk for a long time. Then I stood up and searched around until I found a big rock. I knocked that scythe blade off even with the tree trunk. Then I sat down and cried again.

XXV

I WAS thirteen when Grandpa performed the miracle of the grindstone. It made Grandpa's church famous, not in our town, because it was already famous there, but in big cities as far away as New York and Chicago.

Old Man Jed Isbell caused the miracle. He came down into the valley around '85 or thereabouts. He worked hard and kept his mouth shut, Old Man Isbell did. He took forty acres of flinty land and a mule, and built up one of the nicest farms around Walesburg. For as long as I could remember, Grandpa had been trying to get Old Man Isbell to come to church, but it was no use. Old Man Isbell just claimed he didn't believe in the Gospel. He was almost as tall as Grandpa and he would speak right up to him.

Old Man Isbell had carried a Minié ball in his right

leg ever since the Battle of Chattanooga. I guess I had been to the Isbell place, out on the edge of town, with Grandpa a hundred times and it was always the same. Old Man Isbell always saw us before we reached the frame house sitting under the two big oaks. He would always limp out to meet us.

"Howdy, Parson," he'd say, "light down an' have some of the best well water in the county."

Grandpa's first words always were, "How's that game leg o' yours, Jed?"

For as long as I can remember, the answer was always the same, "Jes' tol'ble, Parson. Jes' tol'ble."

I sometimes used to think that Grandpa thought more of Old Jed Isbell than he did of some of his regular church-goers, but I could never be sure. Especially after we used to leave Old Jed's farm, because Grandpa would get a far-away look in his eyes and look out at the fields and mutter, "That dadburned Jed Isbell, that stubborn pig-headed rebel."

It was always the same. After we'd had some of Jed's iron water and he and Grandpa had discussed crops and the price of cotton, Grandpa would ask, "When you comin' to church, Jed?"

Jed's eyes would get shrewd under their ragged brows. "Jes' as soon as you git God to plow the bottom land for me, Parson."

With that Grandpa would sigh and climb up into the buggy. "Good bye, Jed. Be callin'," and off we'd go.

The pay-off came one hot August afternoon. The sun was bearing down full-force and Grandpa said it was the kind of weather that made a preacher lose his patience. Then, too, Grandpa had other reasons for feeling cranky. The Gailbraith cow had stomped down our vegetable garden, Henry Wallace said the church was going to need a new roof before winter, and a fox had killed one of Grandma's bantam hens.

We stopped by Clem McCollough's to buy some steel traps. Grandpa said he was going to catch that fox or bust. There was a big crowd in Clem McCollough's and right in the middle of it was Old Man Jed Isbell. He was riding sidesaddle on the first store-bought grindstone I had ever seen. I heard it cost Old Man Isbell thirty dollars.

Grandpa was as much taken with that grindstone as anybody else. He hadn't seen Old Jed in more than a month, but he just sort of glanced absently at him. "Howdy, Jed. How's that game leg o' yours?"

"Jes' tol'ble, Parson. Jes' tol'ble," said Jed. You could see he was as pleased as a partridge at all the commotion he was causing. He motioned toward the grindstone. "Give her a try, Parson," and then he stood back sort of show-offish.

Grandpa climbed on the seat and spun the grindstone real fast. He grinned and then climbed down and examined the grindstone real carefully.

"Yes, suh, Jed, that's a real piece o' machinery," he said.

Grandpa and the rest of the men jawed a while about the grindstone and then he told Jed good bye like he usually did. It was automatic, I guess. "When you comin' to church, Jed?"

Old Man Isbell got that shrewd look in his eyes. He lowered his head and looked at Grandpa through his bushy brows and sort of grinned. "When the Lawd starts turnin' this heah grindstone for me, Parson."

Grandpa had already turned away, and I guess any other time he might not have noticed that, but somebody laughed at Old Jed's answer and that brought Grandpa up with a start. He turned around slowly and his eyes were cold. He made that store a pulpit just by drawing himself up to his full height.

"Jed Isbell," he said, and his voice was level, "you mean that after all the Lord has done for you, you would have to see Him turn that grindstone before you'd believe in Him?"

Old Man Isbell was red-faced and embarrassed, but he didn't give ground. "Ah guess that's jes' about the size of it, Parson."

Grandpa studied Old Man Isbell's face for a full minute and everybody in that store sort of got uneasy. My heart was pounding away.

When Grandpa spoke his voice was low. "Hitch up your wagon an' take that grindstone up to mah church, Jed. Then you come to church tomorrow night and I'll see what the Lord will do for you."

There wasn't a sound in that store as Grandpa walked out.

But there was a lot of talking later. It was Saturday and nearly everybody came in Clem McCollough's before the day was over and they heard the story. By nightfall I guess everybody in the valley had heard it.

Down at Jere Higham's place there was all sorts of talk about bets and odds. But of course there weren't any bets made. The only people who would have taken Grandpa's side just weren't the sort of people who gambled.

Grandma heard about what had happened when she went to sewing circle. She came home all wide-eyed and full of wonder, but she didn't seem to know what to say any more than I did. Only Grandpa didn't seem to be thinking about it. He sat in his study quietly all afternoon and when he came to the supper table he brought his silence with him.

Only once did it seem that the conversation was going to get around to what I knew we were all thinking.

"Mister Gray," Grandma began, "what on earth are you . . ."

Grandpa spoke real quickly. "Pass the bread, please."

Grandma tightened her lips and settled back. Grandpa buttered his bread carefully and then he cut his eyes at Grandma and grinned. "We don't cross bridges until we get to them, Harriet."

Grandma just sort of sniffed and then Grandpa chuckled. He finished eating before he spoke again. "The Lord moves in mysterious ways his miracles to perform." He stood up and smiled down at us a second before he left the room.

After I had eaten I wandered out to the front of the house and I was surprised to find that Grandpa wasn't in his study. I looked on the hatrack and saw that his hat was gone. I told Grandma and she was as surprised as I had been.

The clock had just struck nine and I was in my room when I heard Grandpa come home. Grandma met him at the door and then I heard them coming up the stairs together. Grandma must have asked him where he had been because I heard him chuckle and say, "Jest meditatin' with the Lord, Harriet—jest meditatin' with the Lord."

Not since Aunt Pim's funeral had I seen as many people as came to Grandpa's church that Sunday. It was a flat, calm night and the katydids sounded loud as thunder. Folks came from as far away as Millville. I suppose nobody showed up at the other churches in Walesburg. The Baptists and Presbyterians kept off to one side, but you could see that they wouldn't have missed it for anything. Even Old Jere Higham showed up. Guess it was the first time he'd ever been in a church.

When people came into the church, their eyes just naturally went to that big, bright grindstone. It stood right in front of Grandpa's pulpit, and if Old Satan himself had been standing there I guess he couldn't have attracted more attention.

Old Jed Isbell and his family drove up in a wagon. Mrs. Isbell and the girls were sitting in chairs, but Old Jed's oldest son, Rufe, sat on the tail gate. Everybody was looking at the Isbells out of the corners of their eyes, and Old Jed was turkey-red in the face. But his face was determined when he and his family walked down the main aisle of Grandpa's church. There was a lot of neck-craning and glancing going on in that church, but I guess everybody was sort of breathless. I know I was.

Grandpa came down off his pulpit to shake Old Jed's hand. Jed's family sat with the Wheelers, but there wasn't room for him, so he walked down to squeeze into the pew beside me and Grandma.

Grandma and I didn't take our eyes off Grandpa while the choir sang *Rock of Ages*. Then Gussie Lou Liles did a solo, *In the Garden*. I knew Grandpa was nervous, too, because he usually sat quietly during the singing, nodding in time to the music and fanning himself with his big old palmetto-leaf fan. But tonight he sat still with the fan held against his chest.

Then Grandpa got up and explained that the church needed a new roof, and the stewards passed the collection plates while the choir sang softly. Brother Patton made sure he didn't pass up the Baptists and Presbyterians with his plate, and everybody's eyes just about popped out when Jere Higham put a dollar bill on top of all the coins.

I can't remember what Grandpa preached about, and I doubt if anybody else can. That big old shiny grindstone just claimed all our attention. Grandpa paid it no mind. Finally he pulled out his watch, and I knew it was about time for him to stop. He leaned forward over his pulpit with his big hands gripping the edge.

"Friends and neighbors, many of you have come heah tonight to see if God will manifest Himself. Many of you would have come anyway. You always do.

You don't need signs to believe in Him and in His works."

I could just feel that crowd tensing. Old Man Jed's Adam's apple was bouncing, he was swallowing that hard. And it was so quiet you could hear the Gilbert dog barking way down by the river.

Grandpa went on, "I've never been much for callin' on the Lord for miracles. I've been laborin' in His vineyard for more than forty years now, an' I've always wanted to help the Lord 'stead of Him helpin' me. But now I'm goin' to ask for a hand." Then Grandpa threw back his head and said, "Let us pray."

I'd heard Grandpa pray a lot of times, but never like that night. It wasn't one of his thunder-and-lightning prayers, and it wasn't one of his soft gentle prayers.

It was a different sort of prayer, sort of strange, as if Grandpa was asking for forgiveness. While his strong old voice rolled out over that packed church, I got that puffed-up feeling of pride I always felt when Grandpa did something especially grand. I knew then that I didn't care whether that red-and-gold grindstone ever turned or not. I knew then that even if God didn't stand by Grandpa, those people would. You could almost feel their prayers rising. It was that quiet and still and I wasn't afraid any more.

"You sent me a call to go out over this land and preach Your gospel, Lord," Grandpa said, "and ·I will always try to do that. If You can't help me, I know You will be at mah side. I will always be helpin' You."

244

Grandpa stood there with his head thrown back. There wasn't a sound in that church. More than a hundred pairs of eyes followed his finger as he slowly pointed it straight at that old grindstone. We watched, fascinated. Nobody stirred. I could hardly breathe. With every heart thump I prayed, "Lord . . . let . . . it . . . happen . . . Lord . . . let . . . it . . . happen."

A light breeze swept through the church. It made little chills run down my back, sort of like somebody I couldn't see was walking down the aisle of that church.

Then suddenly I thought I saw the far treadle on the grindstone move . . . ever so slow . . . but move! For a second I thought I was mistaken. I blinked my eyes. But then I knew I wasn't wrong. Somebody else had seen it too! I heard a gasp. Then several. The treadle was moving now for certain, slowly, but picking up all the time. The round stone went around, barely moving . . . then faster . . . faster . . . faster.

Somebody sort of sobbed. Somebody else whispered, "My God," but it was a prayer.

That stone still turned. Our throats were dry and our mouths hung open. We were scared. Goose pimples stood out all over me. The stone turned, turned, turned. It was going almost as fast as a full-grown man could pump it.

For some reason I'll never know, I looked from the grindstone to Grandpa. Everybody else had their eyes glued to the turning wheel. Grandpa was sitting in his chair looking like he was seeing a vision, and his eyes were brimming with tears. I looked for just a second, because there was a loud bang and a thump. I looked back to the grindstone. It was flat on the floor. It had been going too fast to stay on its shiny legs.

Nobody moved for a full minute. They just looked at that grindstone like a ground squirrel stands frozen-still when a rattler pins him with his eyes. Then the people began to move like they were just waking up. Awe made most of them sit still with their mouths hanging. But there was a lot of low sobbing, and I heard later that the youngest Wheeler girl had fainted.

Somebody in one of the front pews—one of the Lokey boys, I think—started toward the grindstone.

Grandpa's voice stopped him. "Let it alone," he said. "Leave it there."

Then Grandpa fixed his eyes on Old Jed Isbell, who was as white-faced and stary-eyed as any of us.

"Jed Isbell," he said, and his voice was soft and not a bit braggy, "are you satisfied?" Old Jed gulped and nodded.

Then Grandpa stepped down from his pulpit and looked at the grindstone a long time. He sort of smiled, and everybody just waited, sitting quiet like in a dream. Grandpa finally looked up and swept his eyes across that big crowd until they came to Old Jed. Then his mouth sort of crinkled at the edges.

"Jed Isbell," he said softly, "you're a fool." He said it like a blessing. He nudged the fallen grindstone with his foot. "You're a fool, Jed Isbell, because you let a little red and gold paint and an armful of wood and stone convince you that God loves you.

"Look into your soul, man. What do you see? Do

246

you see Lookout Mountain and the grapeshot buzzin'
around like hornets? There were a lot of good men
with you there, Jed—Ned McDavid, Jeb Ware and
your brother Tom. They stayed there, Jed, stone-cold
and not breathin' God's blessed air. But you—you came
off that mountain, and life was good and sweet." Then
Grandpa lowered his voice. "Think, man, think!
Which is more important—this machine turnin' or God's
gift of life? And do you remember when Rufe got sick
when he was a baby, Jed? How could you forget it?
That little baby turnin' and twistin' in pain. Remember
how you cried, Jed—cried like a man in hell when the
city doctor told you that boy would never walk again?
What do you think now, Jed, when he works in the
fields with you—when you see the muscles workin' in
his strong young body? Tell me, if you dare, man, that
this—this machine spinnin' is more important than that."

Grandpa looked down at the grindstone like it was
a cottonmouth. Then he leaned forward and looked
Old Jed in the eye again.

"And tell me this, Jed Isbell: What do you think
when you drop seeds in the ground, and cotton and
corn pop up? Your sweat and your achin' back can't
help them. But they grow . . . and you know they will.
That's all faith is, Jed—trust in somethin' you can't do
for yourself. You never questioned a seed, did you,
Jed?"

Grandpa's voice was so soft now that people leaned
forward in their seats to hear him. He was speaking
directly to Jed.

"What do you think when you sit down to a full

247

table and look about you into the faces of your wife and children? What is more important—what you see then or what you saw here today? The Lord has been mighty good to you, man, mighty, mighty good!"

I heard a sort of choking sound next to me. I looked at Jed. Big tears were running down his weather-beaten old cheeks. Old hard-boiled Jed Isbell was crying!

But Grandpa wasn't through yet. He let his words sink in a minute. "All your life, Jed Isbell, you've been askin' the Lord to give you something—to show you a sign that He was by your side. All the time He was there so constantly, so close that you took His help as your just due. When people pray, Jed, the first thing they should do when they get off their knees is to roll up their sleeves an' start answerin' those prayers."

Grandpa stepped back, and I could tell by his face that he had some sort of surprise.

"Friends," he said, talking to everybody now, "when you came into this church tonight there wasn't a breeze stirrin'. There is now. I prayed for that breeze. The Lord answered mah prayer. Now I'll show you why."

Grandpa reached down and fumbled around the right treadle of the fallen grindstone.

When he straightened up, he had a long piece of black fishline in his hand. He held the string up high. The string went down into a crack in the floor.

"The far end of this string is tied to our windmill," Grandpa said. "This end was hooked to this grindstone. The wind blew. The grindstone turned. God caused that wind to blow. I don't think it's important that this grindstone turned. If we are to give thanks, let's get down on our knees because the breeze turned windmills all up an' down this valley. The breeze pumped water for our stock. It may bring water to our corn crops. God an' I together turned the grindstone. I had no right to shoulder off the whole load on God."

Grandpa looked at Old Jed and smiled sort of sadly. "Heah's the miracle, Jed—this string, mah two hands . . . an' God!"

I had been sitting open-mouthed while Grandpa spoke. I was almost afraid to look at Old Jed. But I just had to do it. I turned slowly. Old Jed had that mild smile on his face now. He was looking at Grandpa through his bushy brows, but his eyes didn't have that shrewd look in them.

Old Jed stood up slowly. While we all watched, almost scared to breathe, he walked straight toward the pulpit. When Jed reached Grandpa, he stood right in front of him, almost shoulder to shoulder, almost eye to eye, every bit as tall as he was. Then Jed poked out his calloused, old hand and Grandpa took it.

Grandpa smiled. Jed smiled. And God in His high Heaven must have been smiling too. The breeze blew so hard it rattled the windows in Grandpa's church.

XXVI

AFTER that the years fell as softly as the leaves used to drift down from Aunt Pim's old oak. Walesburg didn't grow much, but eventually we managed to see all the signs of progress that were shaping a different world. Some thought it was a better world. It was hard for me to decide. I strode to manhood through those happy years. Pleasant memories clung to me as tightly and as thickly as beggar-lice used to cluster my clothes when I walked through the autumn woods in boyhood.

Grandpa's church became a Mecca for sightseers. They would gather in little hushed groups in front of the pulpit and wonderingly finger a slight depression in the floor that the grindstone had made when it fell.

I remember the first horseless carriage chugging

through the streets of Walesburg. It belonged to Young Doc Harris and on cold mornings he had to prime the spark plugs with ether which he carried in his worn black bag. I was one of the first kids to shout mockingly, "Get a horse! Get a horse!" Later I also was one of the first kids to dream of owning a Stevens-Duryea of my own.

I shook the hand of the great John L. Sullivan. He came to our town and gave a Temperance lecture at Grandpa's church. Afterwards he had dinner at our house. He was the first living legend I had ever met and I was awed and a little frightened. When I tried to tell people about it later, though, all I could remember was his deep, booming voice and his monstrous appetite.

I remember the day three efficient men came and strung wires from poles into our house. Then Grandpa, a bit uneasily, snapped a switch and a small bulb glowed and chased away shadows that had been lurking in corners of our house ever since anyone could remember.

It was almost as exciting as when Clem McCollough put plate-glass windows in his store and everybody gathered to admire them and leave fingerprints on their shining surface.

Most of all I remember when the Presidential Special came puffing into our depot. The president himself came out on the rear platform, showing his big teeth in a dazzling smile and waving his arm vigorously while the Spanish-American War veterans shouted, "We're for ya, Teddy!"

There were thousands of other memories too— small ones that stayed hidden and never rippled my consciousness until I saw a boy playing with his dog, or smelled leaves burning in the fall or heard a phrase which I had used in boyhood. Then these small recollections came out boldly, and wherever I was, whatever I was doing, I paused an instant to fondle them.

During those eventful, jam-packed years I went to many funerals and bowed my head while Grandpa consigned a worn body back to the rich soil in our valley. And I timidly peered into bassinettes at wrinkled, red little mites of humanity who miraculously grew up to play Tar Baby and Hide-and-Seek and shout noisily in the quiet of our long summer evenings. One day I walked self-consciously from the house in my first pair of long trousers. It was hard to say which was stronger, my pride or my embarrassment. I had fights. Sometimes I won and sometimes I lost. And one night—when the very moon itself seemed breathless—I kissed a girl.

I was good. And I was bad. I smoked rabbit tobacco and corn silks and then one day boldly lit a cigar. I was sick. And I was well. I lived from day to day. I grew. I thought. In short, I weathered that sometimes provoking, always delightful period which is known as "growing up."

Then one Indian summer afternoon I sat on the veranda with Grandpa, proud but uncomfortable in the high-collared uniform of a second lieutenant in the Field Artillery. Within a few weeks I was to be in the war which people said would end all wars. But Grandpa and I didn't mention that. We sat silently with our thoughts. The only noise came from the kitchen where

Grandma was bustling around, preparing the last meal I was to have at home for a long time.

Finally Grandpa cleared his throat. "What you plannin' on doin' when you come back from, er, uh— Over There, son?"

I hesitated a minute. Grandpa and I had never discussed my future. I knew that he had always hoped that I would be a minister, but I had known for a long time that I wouldn't. "I've been thinking that maybe I'd like to write," I said.

For some reason I half expected that to surprise Grandpa. If it did, he didn't show it. He seemed to be turning that over in his mind. "What would you write?" he asked.

I laughed. "I haven't the slightest idea," I said. "I thought maybe I'd try to get a job on a newspaper first. Then, later on, maybe I can write something else. I'd . . . I'd even like to try a book."

Grandpa nodded at that, then he sighed deeply and turned in his chair. "Well, son," he said, "I guess you know I've always hoped that maybe you'd be a preacher?"

"Yes," I said, "I knew—but I don't think I was meant to be one."

Grandpa looked at me closely. "You're not ashamed of religion, are you, son?"

I shook my head. "No, sir," I said, truthfully, "I'd be proud to be a minister. When I was small I wanted to be one more than anything." I grinned at the recollection. "I find that a lot easier to understand than I do

253

this sudden desire to write. I don't even know that I can write. Maybe I'll never be able to do it—but I do want to try!"

For just a second I guess my voice sounded intense. Then I looked at Grandpa and I saw he had been studying my face. That soft little smile I knew so well was tugging at the corners of his mouth. "What would you put in your book, son?"

I shook my head again and groped for the right words. "I don't know—really. I've got to see things. I've got to live. I've got to wait until I decide."

Grandpa's voice was mild. "I hope you never write an ugly book, son."

"What do you mean?"

Grandpa chuckled. "Well, son, I think you'll have to admit that some of the books you've been readin' the last few years are hardly the sort of thing you'd take to Sunday School."

I grinned, too, and flushed a little. "But Grandpa, some of those books you call ugly are great books. When you write you must tell things as they are. Successful authors can't always write about sweetness and light."

Grandpa sat quietly and digested this in his mind. When he spoke his voice was still mild. "Maybe you're right—an' I guess I'm up to mah old tricks of bein' a preacher." He looked at me. "But remember this—if you dredge any man's soul you'll find some ugliness hidden away.

"Some writers can look at poverty and see only the wretched details. They forget that poor people can also be happy. They examine love an' see it as something of the flesh. They go out of their way to show that a man in love can be an animal. They seem to forget that true love can be the dearest, cleanest emotion that man has— it's the emotion that sets him apart from the animals rovin' the jungle. If you write, never forget that life can be as sweet as it is bitter."

Grandpa sighed before he continued. "Take Ella Wiley as an example. Some writers would see her as a poor, twisted soul. Yes—an' take your Aunt Pim. They wouldn't have the depth to see something good in her deceit. Take Chloroform Wiggins—what would they do to him?"

Grandpa shook his head, and when he turned again his voice was earnest. "Son, promise me you'll always look for the good things. Some people may accuse you of shuttin' your eyes to the facts, but believe me, you'll be as right as they are. Nobody is wholly good, an' nobody is wholly bad—but I think most people are better than they are bad. If they weren't the human race would have disappeared long ago."

I thought that over for a long time. Finally I nodded. "I'll try," I said.

Grandpa smiled and stood up. "Let's go see if dinner isn't 'bout ready."

That day passed quickly. Almost before I knew it, it was time to go. I held Grandma tight and when she started crying, it reminded me of that morning long ago when I started to school. I tried to comfort her. "Now, now, Grandma," I said, "can't you ever get used to passing milestones."

255

Somehow walking down to the depot with Grandpa also brought back memories of that first day at school. We walked along quickly, not saying a word, but I knew we understood one another. We stood on the depot platform together, both of us feeling a little uncomfortable in that awkward period which invariably precedes good byes. Then my train came hissing into the station. It was time for me to leave. I shook hands with Grandpa, and for the first time a shadow of anxiety clouded his face.

"I want you to promise that you'll pray, son," he said. "As long as you say your prayers you'll be safe."

I nodded. Then I picked up my bag and started away. I hadn't gone three feet before I heard Grandpa's voice. "Son!"

I turned around and Grandpa walked up to me. He was smiling and pride was shining in his eyes.

"Jest because you pray, son," he said, "—that doesn't mean you don't have to keep your hind end down!"

I grinned and shook his hand again—harder this time. Then the old 5:10 blew, and as I swung aboard I couldn't help thinking—my grandpa was a mighty practical man.